Thou Shall Not Judge

By Dr. CI

Acknowledgments

To my ancestors, those divine Black spirits who walk with me whisper wisdom into my bones and remind me daily that melanin is a gift and desire is a birthright. Thank you for teaching me the true meaning of strength, sensuality, and soul-deep love. Your blood runs through these pages.

To Gigi, my editor and literary anchor, thank you for always showing up, even in the storm. Your brilliance and consistency have carried this story and many of my works across finish lines I wasn't sure I could reach. I appreciate you more than words could ever hold.

To my mother and the matriarchs of my family, you are the blueprint. You taught me how to move through this world with softness wrapped in fire. Your lessons in self-love, boundary-setting, and power have sculpted the woman I am. You gave me roots and wings.

To my Uncle Bone, may you rest in power. You taught me authenticity and the beautiful art of not giving a single fuck about anyone who didn't see my worth. You were my rebel saint; your spirit is all over the inspiration for this work.

To my closest friends, you know who you are. Thank you for loving me through every rewrite, every voice note at 1 AM, and every confession that turned into dialogue. You served as muses, mirrors, and medicine. These characters carry your essence, fire, flaws, and beauty. I love you fiercely.

This book is for all of us.
The bold. The bruised. The blooming.

And boo thangs, we are still rising.

Table of Contents

In memory of anybody who showed up as your authentic self in the face of rejection and never wavered. To the activists, advocates, allies, and accomplices fighting for justice. This is for us as you find your true selves on the journey for justice. This book is the first of many, because we have many stories to tell.

With Love and Light,
Dr. CI, aka Dr. Kinky

Chapter 1: The Moment

The sounds of his moans made her want to keep going. The throbbing of her pussy made her want to tell him to stop. The astounding amount of pleasure she felt floating through various parts of her body due to the force being pushed through the girth of his dick made this moment worth it; Aseeka knew precisely what to do when she needed relief from the daily pressures of her work and the escapes of her daily life. "Refocus," she told herself while she tried her damndest not to think about what was on her mind and tried to focus on the caramel, Mandingo-built, 6'4" blessing of a man between her legs. He slowly bent down and started kissing her neck, and the warmth of his mouth and his thick lips brought a simultaneous familiar pleasure to both her mind and body. He knew exactly how to please her and never hesitated to oblige as long as she remained submissive. "Oo, ouch," she moaned out as she felt him push his thick, long, nine-inch, girthy dick as deep as it could go into her tight, wet pussy. She swore she could feel the veins from his dick pulsating against her pussy walls, which made her even wetter. He lifted his head slowly from her neck while running his lips along her cheek, and with his deep brown eyes, he looked down at her and smiled. His pretty white teeth displayed a subtle arrogance rooted in the accomplishment of pleasuring her through pressure and a bit of pain. He slowly started licking her right nipple in a circular motion while pinching the other nipple just enough to induce pleasure. He did this for a couple of minutes; he knew what to do to keep it going, she thought, as her pussy seemed to grow wetter and wetter with every nipple suck. He then lifted his head and glared at her with intense silence while slowly moving his dick in and out of her body. She knew what was coming next and shook with excitement.

She glanced down at his fully-tattooed torso while he took his left hand and grabbed her right wrist from the pillow she was gripping. He repeated the same action with his right hand on her left arm, then fully stretched her arm out over her head and arched his torso over her so that he was fully penetrating her. Then he slowly let go of her wrist, and she knew from the intensity of his eyes that she should not move her hands. He slowly took his hands, slid them down the sides of her body, and elevated his beautifully chiseled caramel frame to a parallel position. He then moved his hands down the outside of her thighs, past her knees, and to her ankles. Slowly, he grabbed both of her ankles and made sure to bend her knees and spread her legs gently where he held them in place as he began thrusting his dick gently in and out of her. He knew his dick was more significant than she was used to, but they had been talking for almost three months now; it was time to introduce her to his favorite body part, he thought, feeling accomplished and confident. "It's time to break your ass in," he said to her with a mischievous smile. All while never breaking eye contact. He could feel her wet, tight pussy pulsating as he began thrusting in and out of her gently at first, but then her moans got louder as he sped up. The sounds of the intensity of her moans, matched with the drumming of his pelvis smacking against hers, were turning him on even more than usual. The juices from her pussy splashing all over his dick enticed him to wonder if she was a squirter. He had made women squirt before, so it wasn't anything new to him; he would conquer her little tight pussy the same as he had done other women's.

Aseeka was in a place of ecstasy; the pressure from his dick moving in and out of her vigorously was bringing her to a place she had never experienced before. She was used to average-size dicks of about five to six inches, but nine inches was stretching her limits. She was ready for the challenge, or so she thought. She could feel him growing in excitement while his pelvic thrust became more intense. Her back was now arching, and she could feel her body heating up. She saw beads of sweat forming on his forehead while he gazed down at his dick sliding in and out of her. He was lost in her in this sexual moment, and he was in complete control. As he intensified the strokes in her pussy she started to feel like the pressure was too much, it was beginning to hurt, but she was torn between pleasure and pain, not knowing if she wanted him to stop. So she tried her best to focus on the pain as tears ran down the side of her face to her ears. She could feel the tip of his curved, long-ass, girthy dick hitting her G-spot over and over again, and her body continued to feel an extreme rush of pleasure. And then it happened. Her back arched, her legs started to shake, and she felt as if she was going to pee, and then without warning, she let out the only sound she could muster up, "Oh my God," as she squirted her pussy juices all over him. He smiled with immense pleasure as he knew she was going to cum, but he wasn't done yet.

While her body was still recovering and shaking, he pulled his dick, soaked and pulsating, out of her and turned her over. With all the energy she had left in her body Asseka confessed, "Wait, please, I'm not ready," and tried to cover her pussy hole from the back as she was now in the doggy-style position.

He said confidently, "So, I'm ready, and so is my dick." He leaned his warm, wet body up against her as he reached over her and grabbed a small pink throw pillow with the words "juicy" on it as he repositioned himself behind her. As he pushed her hand out of the way and slammed his dick right back into her, he began thrusting it intensely in and out of her. Aseeka could feel the soaked cotton and polyester sheets beneath her as it was the only thing she could hold on to try and control the momentum of her body moving back and forth. Her big, size-D titties bounced underneath her while she moaned out in pleasure.

"What's my muthafuckin name?" he asked.

"Damon," she yelled out in pleasure. With that, he smacked her on the left butt cheek and dug in deeper, harder, faster, just fast enough to make her climax again. Aseeka felt her body getting hotter again as his pelvis slammed up against her ass cheeks, and then she heard him say in a much softer, less confident voice, almost high-pitched, "I'm cummin!"

"Me too," she screamed out as they both erupted. She felt his hot cum squirting all over her ass as he completely collapsed onto her backside. Both of them were sweaty, tired, and satisfied. She could feel the hair from his well-trimmed yet patchy beard on her face and his heavy panting. He slowly drifted into sleep. She looked over at him as he snored lightly and almost in a rhythmic pattern, ass naked in her bed.

She glanced at the old-school alarm clock on the side of the bed, and the red numbers on it blinked 12:12 a.m. on the screen. Here she was again, feeling fulfilled yet incomplete. She wondered if sex and inconsistent intimacy were enough to fulfill her needs as she was growing older. She was now a woman in her early 40s, trying to figure out what was next for her. The blinking from the alarm clock reminds her that time is the one constant thing in our lives and doesn't stop for anything. She could feel her anxiety making her mind race, and she had been working with her to observe her thoughts and was trying her best to let them pass as she slowly grew annoyed at the alarm clock. The alarm clock sat heavily on the nightstand, square and sure of itself, like it had somewhere important to be. Its body was dull brass, chipped at the corners, and tarnished with time, but it seemed proud to her nonetheless. Its screen was round and honest, with thick red numbers that didn't pretend to be sleek or modern. The hour and minutes blinked with a soft, deliberate rhythm while the black screen behind the numbers existed more subtly, like it knew something the others didn't. This wasn't the alarm clock that eased you into the morning with chimes or soothing light. No, this clock *meant* it. It reminded Aseeka of her grandmother, from whom she had inherited the clock. Loud, unapologetically authentic, and didn't give a fuck who didn't like what it had to say. When it rang, it sounded like it had been holding a grudge all night, metal on metal, a frantic clamor that tore through dreams like a fire alarm in a library. And yet, something was comforting in its chaos. Something dependable. It didn't care about your mood, meetings, or sleep cycle. It had one job, and every morning, without apology. The damn thing had witnessed all of her sexual escapades and never said a thing and didn't interrupt! It knew exactly when to go off and remind whoever was in her bed to get up and get out! As her thoughts raced through her head, she felt eyes on her, and when she looked over, Damon was lying there smiling as if he had just accomplished a remarkable feat.

He said, "Damn, that was good AF." She responded I didn't even get to get on top or even give you head. "Next time," he whispered. "What time must you be at work in the morning?" he asked.

"At 9 a.m. You can stay the night if you want to," she said.

Damon couldn't accept the offer, reminding her he had to be home to meet his twin teenage boys, who would return from their all-star basketball camp in the morning. He was a single father who loved his children and wanted to make sure he was always there to support them at every moment. "But maybe next time we could get into some of that more kinky shit if you're up for it."

"I have a drawer full of stuff that says I'm up for it; now get out!" she said jokingly. Damon laughed, jumped up, and wore his grey Adidas jumpsuit, socks, and Adidas Swift Run 1.0- size-12 sneakers. He was such a good dresser, always smelled good, and carried himself well, Aseeka thought as she admired him while he dressed. Remembering that he would have to stop by the store and grab a few groceries to prepare breakfast for his boys in the morning, he stated, "I have to run by the store, but I should be in the office around 11 a.m. to hear my first case. I'll see you around the courthouse, your honor. And I'll call you this weekend," he then climbed on the bed and bent over and kissed her on the lips before abruptly making his exit.

"Lock the door on your way out, sir," Aseeka screamed as he ran down the stairs and shut the door. She then grabbed her iPhone 16 and opened her alarm app to automatically turn on her house alarm and lock all the doors as she drifted deeply asleep before preparing for her day.

The alarm clock rang loudly, waking Aseeka up faithfully at 4:30 a.m. daily. Since she was a child, she has always been an early riser. She used to love to get up early in the morning, although it was a routine her mother instilled in her and her siblings that soon became a normality in her life. She reflected on how her entire family had grown up on the same block because her grandmother, the matriarch they called Big Mama, intentionally kept them close to her. Her aunts and uncles lived two houses down, and her grandmother and grandfather lived across the street. Her inherited cousins lived in "the hood village," a term they deemed their neighborhood, which occupied most of the street. It amazed her how the transmutation of transgenerational trauma brought on by the slavery of African people in America was passed down even through proximity. Being forced apart perpetuated a deep need to stay together, and the idea of separation caused frustration among her family, especially her elders. As a child, she didn't quite process her elders' need to protect them and how they equated safeguarding to closeness. She would often hear her mother intentionally keep them in the library and the local African American bookstore that was a five-minute drive from their house. It was also across the street from the local predominantly Black housing projects that they called Hilltop because of its positioning on top of a hill. It became an intellectual safe haven, and the man and his wife who owned it, Mr. and Mrs. Jackson, would always take the time to educate them every time they visited. They would go in curious and always come out with a new lesson, book, or artwork created by people who came from the same experiences as their family, which mattered to them.

For a moment, Aseeka became a bit teary-eyed as she thought about the lessons she had learned so much about intellectualism, achievements often rooted in struggle from her people that inspired and informed her activism. Aseeka usually thought about her weight, not just the weight of her robe or the cases that crossed her bench, but the invisible load inherited from generations of Black leaders who carved space out of nothing. She thought about Harriet Tubman, who moved through the darkness with nothing but faith and fire; Thurgood Marshall, who fought the system from within until it bent; Shirley Chisholm, who demanded a seat at the table and then flipped the damn table over; and so many others whose names never made the headlines but changed the course of history in their homes, communities, and courtrooms. She also learned about often untold figures like Mansa Musa, Margaret Strickland Collins, Nat Turner, George Carruthers, and Denmark Vesey. It was their resilience, their refusal to shrink, and their quest to define freedom on their terms that shaped her. She understood that her success wasn't just her own; it was built on the backs of those who knew the system wasn't made for them and still dared to lead. Every time she sat behind that bench, she answered a call bigger than herself, honoring the lineage of Black brilliance and survival that had quietly and loudly demanded she rise. These reflective moments led her to practice daily affirmations that helped her rise to greatness. Every day, for the first 10-15 minutes of her morning routine, she would practice Melanated mindfulness, repeating the following phrases:

"I am allowed to be myself and show people who I am.
I allow people to show up for me.
I am loving, loved, and lovable.
I don't care if people don't like me; I am always my authentic self.
I attract genuine friendships with people who want the best for me.
My connections with others are steeped in good intentions.
I create space for people to show up for me.
I find strength in vulnerability.

I am stepping into my power.
I inhale my dreams and exhale my fears.
I release what doesn't reciprocate my energy.
I trust the timing of my life.
I find peace through discipline.
I am becoming a better version of myself each day.
My energy is palpable when I walk into a room.
How others perceive me doesn't define me.
I have everything to gain by releasing the grip of shame.
By acknowledging my inner child, I am one step closer to healing.
I accept radical responsibility for creating my dream life.
I am a muthafuckin sexual goddess.
My heart and mind are open and ready for new experiences."

The repetition of these phrases provided a spiritual calmness that allowed her to go into her morning workout routine confidently. First, jogging/walking for three to four miles, often followed by 30 minutes of weightlifting. She worked hard to sustain her 5'9", 190-pound, size-10, chocolate frame, and she would fluctuate between her goal weight of 185 and 190 pounds. Still, she had learned to love her size with the help of her loving mother, who never criticized her weight and used to fend off her uncles and dumb-ass cousins, who would jokingly call her fat and make fun of her for being chunky as a child, not realizing the harm that would cause in the future even though many of them dated larger white women! It would amaze her how her uncle Juney would call her fat and tease her one minute, and then he'd be bringing his almost 300-pound, 5'6" white girlfriend to Big Mama's house the same day! At the time, she didn't have the language to talk about projecting or understand what it was and how people engaged in it, but now she understood. She had to stop thinking about it when working out because she worked hard to transform her mind that her fitness journey was about health, not an attempt to fit a societal stigma of beauty.

After her workout, she would get ready at the gym. She had a personalized locker she had purchased that consisted of her extra gym outfits, often purchased from Fenty and Actively Black, because fuck a Lulu Lemon. It also had extra clothes, her hair essentials, and grooming needs. Her mother had instilled in them how necessary it was to support Black-owned businesses at a young age; entrepreneurs and activists raised her. The importance of the circulation of the Black dollar in the Black community was ingrained in her from the time she began receiving allowances and making her own money. She could remember her mother and father saying, "Spend your money where you are appreciated. Don't be out here supporting the descendants of your ancestors' enslavers. Until they reciprocate, we will not participate." She could recall the deep voice of her father making that statement. It was one of the many memories she had of him before he was incarcerated when she was four years of age. She never fully understood what happened, but she remembered coming home, and he wasn't there to greet her and her siblings after school one day. Her mother didn't speak much about their separation but also never spoke ill of her father and always spoke of forgiveness and acceptance if she ever saw him again. It was their family mystery, but she would soon uncover details that would rock her fucking existence. She got dressed at the gym, which was two blocks north of the courthouse. She was going to her 2024 emerald-green Range Rover when she heard a male voice yelling, "Aseeka, hold up." She turned her head around to see that Byron was quickly approaching her. She immediately became annoyed as Byron was a regular jump-off for her friend Tasha, whom he treated like his personal trophy side piece. He and Tasha had been dealing with each other off and on for almost 10 years since her friend had divorced her husband. He was a local underground club owner of a spot called Climax, which became a swinger club after hours and was invite-only. That's where he and Tasha had met. Tasha loved a good orgy. Aseeka loved great sex just as much as the next freak but wasn't interested in fucking random people, so she judged Byron for his professional pursuits. He was a well-built man and a member of her fancy gym. He worked out daily and saw her there regularly. She would often see him engulfed in sweat, listening to his music in his Beats by Dre headphones, while dressed in top-notch fitness outfits that complemented his 6'2", muscular, tatted-ass body. Byron knew women found his caramel, athletic ass attractive; he was a pretty humble guy, though. He played point guard in professional basketball for 15 years before he retired. He was a brilliant brother who knew how to invest his money and was community-centered. But his club didn't discriminate; it welcomed people of all genders, shapes, and sizes. She would often hear about the threesome escapades between him and Tasha in grave detail from her friend. She tried not to think about how Tasha would describe his big ass dick and how he knew what to do with it as he was running up to her in his white tank top and grey sweatpants. She thought to herself, "This fool knows exactly what he is doing, running like that, and his dick just swinging!"

"What's up, girl? You are looking good," he murmured, giving her an intense once-over. She could smell his Burberry cologne as she conjured up the discipline to not stare at his bulge. She thought, if the muthafuckin' thing looks that soft, what is it giving when it's hard? She immediately shook off the thought because she was not the type to sleep with her friends' men or anybody they messed with. She stuck by the code!

"Boy, what the fuck do you want? And make it quick. I got shit to do and people to see!" she stated.

"Speaking of seeing, when will we get you out to the club? You know you have to come to experience it at least once," he said enthusiastically. She had heard that the club was lit and was doing well, and they were planning to open another location in Los Angeles in the coming months, which he immediately confirmed. "We are having our grand opening of the spot in LA in a few weeks, and I'd love to fly you and Tasha out, put y'all up in a nice hotel, and have y'all be a part of the celebration. I'm sure Tasha told you about it. I already told her I wanted y'all to come."

She was aware of this as Tasha had sent her the flyer that had the beautiful chocolate ass big booty, thick-ass black chick on it through a text message a few weeks ago. She was dressed proactively in a minidress with lingerie underneath with big ass letters that read, Climax, is Cumming to Your City.

"You mean the freak-off. You know I don't get down with you and your little sex parties, sir!" she said sarcastically.

"Ok, look, I ain't trying to have anybody do anything they don't want to," he said smirkingly. "My facility is all about consent! You could just come and be a spectator. Just think about it and don't be so gotdamn judgy your honor!" he said as he handed her a sleek black and gold envelope. Aseeka took the envelope and admitted that it was elegant and pretty. "I hope to see you there!" he yelled as he jogged back to his lavender colored 2024 Bentley Continental GT Convertible. "And go wash your gotdamn car! Stop neglecting your Bentley, baybeeee," he yelled.

"Boy, fuck you! I have a detailer come to get it this afternoon," she yelled. She was mad, and he called out to her dusty luxury vehicle. "I do need to wash this muthafucka, though," she giggled as she got in her car. She turned on the radio and waited for her iPhone to sync with her CarPlay. Then, she immediately heard the sounds of Jeera, the hot new artist whose Spotify playlist she had downloaded earlier that day. The sounds of her empowering single, "I'm Me," rang out over the speakers as Aseeka started her car and headed to work.

Chapter 2: Werk at Work

Aseeka pulled into her reserved parking space in the Illinois State Courthouse garage, and her phone immediately rang. It was Tasha, and she knew exactly what she was calling to talk to her about. She ignored the call and sent a custom auto-text message that she was at work and would call her on her lunch break.

"Hey, sir, set a reminder for me to call Tasha back at lunchtime," she stated, knowing she would get busy and might forget to call her friend. She was trying her best to fight the urge to attend the party. She knew Byron and his team practiced discretion, and everybody had to sign an NDA, but she was still worried. She had never attended anything like that, but she had to admit that she was intrigued. She couldn't stop thinking about it since Tasha had brought it up. She then glanced at herself in the rearview mirror and said, "Get it together, bitch, you got work to do."

She swiftly exited her SUV and hit the alarm button as she walked through the door leading to the elevator. As she entered the courthouse, she approached the area where she would have to pass through metal detectors to access the elevator. She nodded politely at the security guards, who had long grown used to her quiet, commanding presence. The scent of coffee, polished wood, and tension lingered in the air, a familiar cocktail of the justice system at work. As she passed through the metal detectors and into the buzzing corridors, her face settled into the measured calm of someone who knew that every step she took inside these walls mattered. "Time to get to work and make sure justice is served," she said as she hit the button to go up to the eighth floor to go to her chambers.

Aseeka adjusted the strap of her sleek leather Yvonne Koné bag as she approached the floor leading to her office, the morning air crisp against her skin. The temperature in the building was exactly how she liked it; it was in the mid-60s, and it was pushing 75 degrees outside. She entered the office and saw Ms. Ellie sitting at her desk, ready to greet her with court files and a morning tea, not just the kind of tea you drink. Ms. Ellie was one of her favorite people in the world. A 4'11", no-nonsense, 60-year-old Black woman who didn't take shit from anybody. She would speak of tales about the brown paper bag test she had to undergo when joining her sorority back in the day, and how she fought for the rights of all shades of Black women to be accepted into the organization. Ms. Ellie was a light-skinned woman who loved her people and had put up with the bullshit of sexist white male judges who came through the office for years, but she always outlasted them! She was a wise elder and kept Aseeka in line because even though she always greeted her with a smile, she had no problem getting people together if they came into the office tripping. She was ecstatic when Aseeka was voted into office and looked forward to supporting her through her tenure. Aseeka was the reason she decided not to retire. She had been in the office as the leading judicial assistant to every judge who came through the office for the last 30 years. She had been with Aseeka for 10 years and hadn't aged. Her young spirit kept her witty and sharp, and she always greeted Aseeka with the biggest smile. Ms. Ellie kept her hair and nails done and loved it when her husband would bring her lunch, which he did once or twice a week. She had been married for 30 years before she lost her husband in a tragic boating accident. She remarried five years ago at age 55 and still travels the world with her new husband, Khalil, and they are very much in love. It gave Aseeka hope that she could still find authentic love at an older age, and she constantly reminded her not to give up on love. "Good morning, Your Honor," she said with that big, beautiful smile. She always greeted Aseeka by her title; she preferred it that way, even though Aseeka told her she was more than welcome to call her by her name. "I have all of your case files on your desk, your morning tea heating up, and I ordered your acai smoothie from the cafeteria. It's going to be a long ass day. Let me know if you need anything. And that damn Damon has been creeping around here, working my nerves, walking his tall bow-legged but past here slowly to see if you arrived yet," she said with a smirk. "Your first meeting is in 40 minutes. Do you need me to delay it, or will you be ready?

"I'll be ready. Thank you, Ms. Ellie," she said.

"You welcome, your honor," she replied.

Aseeka placed her hand on the door scanner to her private chambers. She had a private security system installed once she started as an extra security measure because she did not want anybody in the chambers besides her. She often dealt with high-profile cases with highly sensitive information and wanted to be intentional about her security and the materials she had in her office. She knew some shady people could be in the judicial system and did not play with her privacy.

When the door opened, she immediately smelled the scent of the Egyptian cotton incense she had burned the previous day.

It was a beautiful spring day in Chicago, and she could feel the breeze as she opened the small window behind her desk. She could feel the air against her short pixie cut as it ran up her back.

The towering columns she could spot from her view of the front of the courthouse and the weathered façade greeted her like an old, unflinching friend, solid, unmoved by the chaos that often unfolded inside. She moved with purpose, her heels tapping rhythmically against the marble floor as she crossed the office floor to her private restroom. Her best friend, Chanel, a fantastic interior designer, designed her chambers. She was proud of the outcome; it felt like her home away from home. The mood was a whole vibe, equal parts sanctuary, power chamber, and curated Black excellence. The lavender walls softened the sharp edges of her workday, casting a calm, almost regal glow over the space. Anchoring the room was a massive dark marble desk, calm and commanding like her stare when a lawyer tried her in court. Behind it, a wall of heavy law books stretched nearly to the ceiling; some cracked open, others pristine, all testaments to the decades she'd spent mastering the game.

Above the shelves, her degrees from Northwestern and Georgetown hung in sleek black frames, unapologetically on display like war medals. But what made the space sing wasn't the pedigree; it was the soul. Classic Black art by legends like WAK adorned the walls, every canvas bursting with color and movement, unapologetically Black, bold, and beautiful. Between the paintings were photos of her tribes, smiling snapshots of family cookouts, girls' trips with her ride-or-die friends, and a rare, candid picture of her and her father before the world fell apart.

In the corner located to the left of her desk sat an adult-sized, fuchsia lived-in Telfar tote bag that could easily double as a survival kit; inside, you'd find everything from case files, emergency money and credit cards, maxi pads, handcuffs, lip gloss, curling irons to an emergency protein bar. And in the back corner, because Aseeka didn't just talk about self-care, she lived it, sat a Peloton bike, usually occupied during her late-night reading sessions when the weight of justice sat too heavy on her shoulders. Next to the bike was her meditation station, which consisted of Tibetan bowls and crystals that she used when she felt anxious or disturbed to help her recenter. She kept a small portable speaker that would play binaural music or blast anything from Snoh Alegra, Sade, Anita Baker, Lil Wayne, or Twista, depending on how she felt. A lavender-and-white yoga mat was rolled up neatly beside it because she knew the law wasn't the only thing that needed balancing. A custom walk-in closet was built seamlessly into one wall, doors always slightly ajar, revealing racks of designer suits and red-bottom heels, each piece curated to slay both in court and life. It also held her judicial robes, which she had deemed "the black robe of justice." A delicate incense holder sat on her desk, tucked between crystal paperweights and a few open case files, the faint scent of sandalwood she attempted to mask with her incense, always dancing in the air to soothe the edge of legal warfare. She also had a plush grey throw rug in the middle of the floor, which was positioned in front of her portable electric fireplace; she needed a slight touch of something sexy. It was also the first place in the office that she and Damon decided to engage in an intense 69 encounter one late night after an intense deliberation. That rug serves many purposes, but that is the one she remembers the most. It was where she realized for the first time that she was a squirter and where she decided to swallow Damon's cum for the first time, which to her surprise, tasted pretty sweet; his pescatarian lifestyle had come in handy. She smirked as she replayed the moment in her head and could hear the sound of his moans encouraging her to go in on his fine ass. Her thoughts were immediately interrupted by a knock on her door; she pressed the entry button on the bottom of the desk and entered Ms. Ellie. You have 15 minutes before you have to be in the courtroom, and Damon is here to see you," she stated as if she wanted to say, "this nigga outside,"

"Ok, thank you, please send him in," she said as she giggled.

"I was just thinking about you; what's up?" she said. They always tried to keep it professional, especially when Ms. Ellie was in the office. She looked Damon over and admired how the earth tones he was wearing complemented his chocolate skin. He was rocking a light brown Dior suit, complementing his Hermès deep sneaker, leather, Beige/Natural shoe wear. He also rocked a Tissot T-Classic dream brown leather strap watch on his right wrist. She could smell his Tom Ford cologne as she stared at his diamond V-cut platinum necklace hanging just below the crest of his neck. He was looking good as usual.

"Not much; I just wanted to tell you good morning and see if you were prepared to hear your first case," he said.

She quickly thought he always ensured she was ok, not like he was fathering her. Damon had this natural, provider, and caring yet stern energy that she liked about him; she wondered if she ever reciprocated it enough. She reflected on how he shared that his wife had passed five years ago as the result of a drunk driver crashing into her car at the gas station. He was in the station with their two twin boys, getting snacks they had planned to sneak into the movie to watch the newest Disney flick. He briefly talked about how they had been married for 13 years, but he didn't talk much about his emotional state during the time of her passing. She wondered how a 39-year-old man carried such a weight but never wore it on his sleeve. It attracted her even more to him, but she also wanted to nurture him. She didn't understand why, but she always hoped he'd open up one day. So she got up from sitting on her desk, walked over to him, and hugged him, wrapping her arms around his thick neck and placing her sized D cups against his tatted chest.

"Mmmhmm," he groaned out in his deep, sexy-ass voice.

"Yeah, I'm ready, and thank you for checking on me. I'm always grateful when you do that, and I hope you know that," she said as she stared deeply into his eyes. She could smell the mint oil on his breath as he breathed out. He was particular about his breath, and she loved that because lord knows she had gotten rid of men in her past relationships due to consistent funky-ass breath issues they refused to resolve. Like damn brotha, take ya ass to the dentist, why don't you! Damon didn't have that problem, and she loved that about him.

"Do you need anything before you go out there?" he said as he whispered seductively in her ear.

"No, I'm good, but will I see you this week? I know the boys have an AAU basketball tournament," she said quickly, gently kissing him on the lips. His 17-year-old twins were McDonald's All-Americans, graduating at the top of their class. He was doing a fantastic job raising them, and they loved their father. It often made her reflect on becoming a parent, maybe even a stepmother one day, but she and Damon never made anything official. She felt he was still in recovery from his wife's passing, and she didn't know if she was completely ready to settle down into that life. They both loved what they were and never really asked the other about each other's business. She often wondered if this were the story she would tell herself to cope with the fact that Damon said he didn't know if he'd ever remarried, and his boys were his priority. She didn't have any problem with those feelings. But she'd lie to herself if she didn't consider what it would be like if they were in an official relationship. She also enjoyed her freedom; she wasn't out there fucking anybody else but found solace in the fact that she had options because they were not monogamous.

"Yeah, I will come through while the boys are at practice. It should be around 6 p.m. My last case ends around 3 p.m.," he said.

"Ok, cool, I'm done at the same time and will text you when I leave here," she said. She took her arms off his neck and watched him exit as he winked before he closed the door. She walked around and got ready to sit down and review the brief she had studied the day before leaving the office.

Then she heard a loud shout, "10 minutes, Your Honor!" from Ms. Ellie.

"Ok, ma'am!" she responded. She got up, walked to her closet, and put on her black robe of justice as she stared at the mirror inside her closet door. "On my mama, on my hood, I look fly, I look good," she sang out, admiring her armor before she returned to her desk and grabbed her briefs.

The sound of the gavel cracking against polished wood sliced through the tension like a blade.

"All rise," the bailiff announced, voice booming through the marble-paneled courtroom.

Judge Aseeka Sinclair didn't bother looking up immediately. She'd learned long ago that real power wasn't in volume; it was in stillness, in making people wait. She let the silence stretch, the room holding its breath, before finally raising her gaze from the case files.

The defendant stood like most did: small, shaking, already defeated. This one, a crooked CEO who thought his money could buy his way out of accountability, had smirked through the entire trial. But there was no smirk now, just sweat and regret as she gazed down at this cocky, white-collared criminal asshole who loved to steal other people's hard-earned money. His 5'7", small frame, was dressed in a blue Oasi cashmere suit, which he probably brought with him the money he stole from his clients and employees. She could see the tiny beads of sweat forming on his carrot-top hairline. She stared deeply into his blue eyes, ready to deliver justice to this corporate thug. She could see the entitlement all over his face and the face of his lawyer, Joe Orivia, a well-known defender of corporate criminals. She couldn't be too mad at Joe; he was great at his job and worth the 250K retainer he paid his clients upfront.

Aseeka adjusted her black robes, smoothed the sleeve, and spoke in that rich, clear tone she'd mastered over years of being underestimated.

"Mister Carmichael, you stand before this court convicted of fraud, embezzlement, and exploitation of workers in underserved communities. Your actions weren't just criminal. They were predatory."

Her eyes flicked up, dark and unreadable. "And you will serve ten years without the possibility of parole."

The gavel hit the block again, final and unforgiving.

The murmur in the courtroom sounded like waves crashing against rock. Aseeka ignored it. She had a full day of rulings, back-to-back meetings, and a night that would likely end the way it always did, alone in her penthouse, a glass of bourbon in hand, scrolling past text messages she wouldn't respond to.

She gathered her papers, ready to disappear into her chambers, when her clerk approached quietly.

"Judge Sinclair, your next docket assignment just came through. The Garvin case."

Something in her gut twisted; I know that name. She glanced at the file in her hand.

People vs. Dr. Leonard Garvin.
Charges: Sexual misconduct, assault, abuse of power.

The trial was scheduled in two weeks. A sinking, sickening feeling rose in her throat.

She knew that name. Knew it too well. She knew it like a shadow she'd never told anyone about.

Her hands tightened around the folder as she whispered to herself: "Not him."

Chapter 3: The Gwerls + 1

After a full day of sentencing corporate criminals and delivering justice, Aseeka was ready to hit the streets with her girls. She had gotten home just enough time to host homie happy hour from 4-6 before Damon would slide through around 7 p.m. She lived in a penthouse in a secure building located in Hyde Park. Aseeka loved the water and was big on views, so she had to be able to see Lake Michigan and listen to the sounds of the water and let them soothe her soul after a long ass day.

Aseeka's penthouse was perched just high enough to catch the sun sliding across Lake Michigan like melted gold. Floor-to-ceiling windows wrapped the space in light, her decor minimalist but intentional, with deep jewel tones, curated art, and books stacked like altars. From her balcony, she could see joggers weaving through Promontory Point and the shadows of downtown flirting with the horizon. It was Hyde Park at its finest: old money meets new power, with just enough soul. Aseeka Sinclair's penthouse was a study in restraint, precision, and seduction. A modern Japanese aesthetic anchored the space, clean lines, uncluttered surfaces, and a reverence for stillness that mirrored her desire for control. Every element was intentional. The color palette? A high-contrast symphony of black and white, with curated accents of deep, blood-red, just enough to whisper danger, desire, and power.

The open-concept living area flowed effortlessly from room to room, punctuated by low-slung black furniture with angular silhouettes. A plush white sectional stretched beneath the window facing Lake Michigan, its fabric smooth and cool. In front of it sat a lacquered black coffee table adorned with a single, deep red orchid and a stack of rare photography books, each cover as provocative as her own secrets.

Japanese shoji screens, reimagined in sleek black matte wood with translucent panels, stood like sculptures in the corners, dividing space without obstructing the natural light. The floors were a soft charcoal tatami-style tile, warm underfoot, and whisper-quiet, perfect for barefoot walks after long days in court.

Art was everywhere, but not just any art. Large-format Black photography and paintings by artists like Awol Erizku and Mickalene Thomas adorned the walls. One piece, a Black woman reclining nude, head thrown back in ecstasy, lips parted in prayer or pleasure, hung near the bedroom door, daring anyone who entered to look deeper. Another depicted a couple in silhouette, wrapped in a tangle of limbs and smoke, powerful and tender at once. These weren't just decorations; they were declarations of seduction. In the kitchen, high-gloss black cabinets contrasted with white marble countertops veined in subtle silver. A strip of deep red LED lighting glowed underneath the island, casting a sultry warmth in the evenings. A red cast iron teapot sat beside her espresso machine, a quiet nod to ritual and routine.

The bedroom was pure seduction. A platform bed with black satin sheets and a headboard carved with minimalist Japanese waves dominated the space. Hanging pendant lights replaced traditional lamps, glowing like soft lanterns. A floor-to-ceiling mirror stood across from the bed, and at the foot, a black leather bench rested with a folded red kimono-style robe tossed over it like an invitation. On the wall above the bed: a single, massive canvas, a Black woman's face mid-laughter, mid-moan, mid-liberation.

Everything smelled like her: lavender vanilla, oud, and something slightly floral. The air was calm but charged, like a thunderstorm waiting to break from chaos to breathe.

Aseeka sat at the corner of the rooftop patio, legs crossed, wine glass in hand, surrounded by the only people in the world who made her feel like she could finally breathe.

The wine flowed, the charcuterie board was half-devoured, and Malik's playlist was a sinful mix of Jill Scott, Summer Walker, and City Girls.

Tasha was halfway through telling a story about cussing out her son's teacher when Brielle rolled her eyes, already tipsy and too polished to listen to Tasha's brand of hood gospel.

"I told that woman," Tasha said, gesturing wildly, "you call me again about my baby chewing gum in class. I'm pulling up. And not in no PTA meeting way."

Laughter cracked across the patio like thunder.

Aseeka smiled, the corners of her mouth pulling, but her mind was somewhere else, still stuck in that cold courtroom, staring at the name on that file.

Chanel leaned over, always the quiet observer. "You've barely touched your wine. What's up with you tonight?"

Malik slid into the conversation, legs crossed elegantly, sipping his rosé. "Yeah, what's got Judge Judy over here looking like somebody canceled her Pornhub subscription?"

Aseeka laughed, soft and hollow. "Work."

Brielle narrowed her eyes. "Work's always a mess, but tonight your energy feels … rattled."

Aseeka shrugged, trying to fold her walls back up before they noticed too much. She loved and hated how much her lifelong friends knew her, but she also appreciated the concern for her well-being because shit was feeling heavy ass fuck, "It's a case. Someone I used to know."

The table fell quiet for a second, the energy shifting.

Tasha's brow arched. "Someone you used to know … like how? Friend? Foe? Ex?"

"Doctor," Aseeka said casually, swirling her wine. "I knew him in my 20s He was my and my mother's gynecologist."

Sydnie tilted her head, studying her. "And …?"

Aseeka shook her head, forcing a smirk. "Nothing to tell. Just … funny how people from your past resurface."

Brielle exchanged a look with Malik, who mouthed, *Bullshit.*

But no one pressed. They knew Aseeka's walls were titanium. She'd talk when she was ready or when she broke.

Tasha raised her glass. "Well, whoever he is, fuck him. And here's to Black women staying paid, booked, and unbothered."

Malik laughed, "And men nigga, just cause I'm gay don't mean you only get to acknowledge the Gwerls!"

Laughing loudly, Aseeka, who was also feeling tipsy from her Japanese whisky, blurted out, "Don't start that shit tuhday!"

Tasha decided to claim the attention of the moment: "I don't know if y'all remember, but today is the five-year anniversary of the day I signed my divorce papers and my marriage ended."

Sydnie, whom they all referred to as Syd, stated, "Yeah, I remember," as they reached into the Louis Vuitton bag and pulled out the same bottle of Veuve Clicquot La Grande Dame Rose & Clos Colin Champagne Set. "I brought this for you today like I did the day I watched your heartbreak and begin healing all at the same damn time."

Syd was the group's poet and a popular singer-songwriter who made music that focused on uplifting their community. Syd started out as Sydney and transitioned at the age of 19 into their authentic self. The friends admired Sydney's journey and courage to bet their authentic self, coming out as gay at the age of 15 and didn't give a fuck what anybody thought. Their parents had them in boxing since they were 7, and their father was a Krav Maga black belt who taught his children how to defend themselves as soon as they could throw a punch. They also went on to earn the Golden Gloves in boxing at the age of 18. Sydney stood 5'11" without heels, 200 lbs., with about 8 percent body fat, but had the nicest titties, compliments of Dr. Shinga, a cosmetic legend in the LGBTQ+ community. Syd had to fly to New York for those D cups, but it was worth the trip. They all accompanied them on the trip, because if and whenever you needed Syd, through rain, sleet, or snow, they showed the fuck up.

Aseeka loved Syd dearly and often reflected on how they had always been a protector of her since they met in middle school. She always vowed to be the same for Syd and had to learn what it meant to be an accomplice of justice for the trans community, especially growing up in a Christian, homophobic family. She knew more about justice at an early age from Syd's experience than any of her other friends. Her family claimed they loved all people regardless of sexuality, but the microaggressions showed something different. Watching them go through rejection, the ignorance of other children and adults, and the rejection from certain family members. Syd's parents were somewhat supportive and loved their child through it all, but they struggled initially to understand. Their mother's Black hippie ass had no problem defending her child at any cost but still struggled to get the language right, the concepts, and even the change in clothing, makeup, etc., but didn't hesitate to attend makeup classes with her child. Her father was uncomfortable with it all at first but attended therapy with his child to try to understand it all. Yet, he still wouldn't hesitate to put his hands on anybody who fucked with his baby. He knew that his child would be up for a struggle due to the ignorance and hate in the world, so he gave them what he could to make sure they could protect themselves, both mentally and physically, throughout their lives.

Syd said with a deep conviction, "I remember sitting next to you at that arbitration table, ready to kill that cheating ass narcissistic muthafucka if he disrespected you as he had done so many times before."

Tasha's eyes softened a bit. "I'm not bitter about it, and honestly, I don't think about it much anymore. I appreciate how it taught me to heal and how my kids have a good relationship with their father. We're at a place of being cordial and co-parenting well. Plus, I'm having the best sex of my life! Cause that Byron dick is something different y'all."

They all raised their glasses, laughing loudly, "Ayeeeee," the moment lightened again.

"Plus that $10 million settlement, two properties, and a seven-figure accounting business that stays in the black mind you, that you got to keep didn't hurt!" Chanel said enthusiastically.

"Cheers to that bish!" screamed Tasha as she raised her champagne glass and looked across the table at Syd. "You always know how to cheer me up. I love you boo."

Syd smiled and said softly, " I love you too, sugah!"

Bri chimed in as she sipped her Moscato, "Yeah, but being married does have its benefits when it's good. I enjoy the in-house dick and the supportive partner, and my lil ol' family.

"Don't nobody care!" said Chanel, smirking.

Aseeka fired at Chanel, "Don't be mad at her cause your husband is an asshat and Kenneth isn't. You picked that fool, and most of us are still wondering what the fuck is up with that!"

Their friendship had always been built on authenticity and clear communication, but they respected each other's boundaries while calling each other on their bullshit.

Brielle, whom they called Bri, was happily married to Kenneth, and they had three children. They had been together since high school, and Kenneth was a very private but loving person. He supported Bri's pursuit of being a fashion designer and even built her first boutique. They owned a private architectural firm and had an ideal life. Sure, it had challenges, but they were happy and had a good life.

Chanel, on the other hand, married Markee, whom she had dated seriously for two years before he went to prison for three years for drug trafficking. He had gotten caught trying to pass the Canadian border with medication to help his mother overcome the high prices of insulin that she couldn't afford. The entire group told her to wait until he was released, but Chanel felt she was in love, so she married him while he was locked up. Aseeka always felt that he was wrongfully imprisoned; she knew the story of Black men and the education-to-prison pipeline all too well. To be honest, if he weren't such a dickhead to Chanel, she would've pulled some strings to try to get his record expunged. Every now and then, she considers it, but once she interacts with him, she changes her mind. Although it was his first and only offense, if she helped him out, it might help his attitude. Then again, she had to work on her hero complex and want to save every damn body because that hadn't always worked in her favor. She had been planning to sit down and talk to Chanel about it; she made a mental note to follow up about it later in the week.

Chanel fired back, "Y'all tired asses goin stop judging me; I am determined to make my marriage work."

"No, we not," Malik said snarkily as he sipped whisky and peeked over the glass at Chanel with judgmental eyes.

They all got quiet for a second and burst into laughter. Malik leaned over. "Oooh, this is my song," he said as he turned up the volume on his phone, and Jodeci's "Come and Talk to Me" sounds rang out over the speakers.

But as the music swelled and the laughter resumed, Aseeka sat quietly, her smile a little too tight, her mind a thousand miles away. She came back to reality again when her phone went off. She picked it up to find an iMessage from Damon that read, "On the way," with a devilish emoji. She already knew what time it was and had to put everyone out to prepare.

"Ok, peeps, happy hour over, y'all gotta go, get to steppin'!" she said while getting up from her chair.

"That must be that Damon, I'm coming to get that pussy alert," Tasha said with enthusiasm, "Y'all know what time it is, let's head to Limelight for a round of drinks on me."

Aseeka said, "How y'all goin' to our favorite spot without me? That's not fair!"

"Chile, please, you putting us out for that fine ass mule of a man is not fair. Can I hide in the closet and watch? I know y'all be in here doing unspeakably nasty shit," Malik said with widened glossy eyes and pure excitement. He grabbed his Gucci fanny pack and gestured for the girls to head to the door. "Let's go run up Tasha's tab at Limelight bitches."

Tasha said sarcastically, "I seriously need richer friends; I hate you broke bitches."

"We hate you too, now grab your Louis purse and your Louis wallet and come the fuck on," said Syd. as they pushed Tasha to the door.

"Get out of here; we're still on for brunch Sunday, yes?" Aseeka said as opening the door.

"Yasssss," they all muttered in unison.

Malik resisted being the last one out the door and swiftly turned his head to Aseeka. "Are you sure you don't want me to watch from the closet?" He said jokingly, and with a bit of seriousness.

Aseeka chuckled while pushing him by the middle of his back, "Y'all text the group chat when y'all get home; you know the routine." She shut the door.

"Bitch!" Malik yelled from the other side.

"Shut up and go take shots!" she said. After she locked the door, she knew she had about 20 minutes to prepare for Damon's arrival. She ran up the stairs and darted straight for her costume closet. She loved "role play Fridays," she had something new for his ass.

"It's go time," she said, pulling out her sheer judge's robe.

Chapter 4: Submissive in Robes

Aseeka's penthouse was quiet except for the soft hum of the jazz playlist she kept on when she couldn't sleep. The city lights outside her floor-to-ceiling windows blinked like restless stars.

She was pouring her second glass of bourbon when her phone buzzed. Damon was about 30 minutes late, which was usual as he navigated traffic in the Chi on a Friday night. Plus, she lived in a live area with foot traffic at night, so she wasn't trippin'.

Damon: *You still up?*

She didn't respond right away. She didn't need to. She knew that he knew the drill. She wanted to make him feel like he was in trouble, and he loved being "in trouble." Five minutes later, there was a knock at her door.

Damon stepped into Aseeka's penthouse, already knowing he was in trouble. The scent of Black love incense filled the air, and the heat from the fireplace wrapped around him like Aseeka's thick-ass chocolate thighs. The fireplace was turned down low, making the room dark with minimal lighting. The only light in the place came from the warm red glow under the kitchen island and the flicker of tea candles scattered like breadcrumbs leading toward the room Aseeka had turned into her home office. He slowly took off his shoes, giddy with a small child's excitement.

She stood in the center of the room in her black Jimmy Choo stiletto sandals, legs gleaming, and her sheer robe open just enough to reveal the outline of red lace barely covering her skin resting on her thick body. Her hair was flawlessly styled in a pixie, curled to a T, and on top of her head like a crown, and the look in her eyes said this wasn't going to be a negotiation. Aseeka stood in the low red glow of her bedroom, the subtle scent from her Victoria's Secret warm vanilla lotion and spray hitting Damon's nose; that shit turned him on. It was his favorite scent. Just the smell of it could send the blood rushing into his big Black, veiny ass dick. He immediately gave her a once-over; he felt his bulge begin to form. He was ready to be sexually submissive, and he graveled at her presence, which was both holy and wicked. She held a black leather flogger in her hand, its braided handle gripped loosely, the strands swaying like a dark promise. She let the tails brush gently against her bare thigh as she walked, slow and deliberate, each step a silent command.

The flogger wasn't raised. Not yet. She let it hang at her side, dragging it across her palm, then up the line of her stomach, teasing her own skin like foreplay. Her eyes locked on her lover's calm, controlled, but burning with intent. She made it clear with a slight tilt and the curl of her full lips: *this was not a game.*

She brought the flogger to her mouth, lips parting just enough to let the leather graze her tongue, wetting it with slow, decadent ease. Then, she whispered, "Do you know what this feels like? Soft ... until it isn't."

She stepped closer, letting the strands fall gently across his chest, over his thighs, watching him twitch in anticipation.

"You want it?" she purred. "Beg for it. Like a man who knows he's guilty."

And just like that, the judge became the executioner, elegant, merciless, and divine.

"Strip," she said, no greeting, no smile, just command.

He froze for a second. "Aseeka—"

"I said *strip,* Counselor."

His mouth went dry. He slowly pulled his white T-shirt over his head, watching her every move as she walked over to the built-in closet and pulled out a black silk tie. Then another. Then another. She tossed them onto the floor without a word and turned back to him.

"Hands," she said softly.

He held them out.

She tied his wrists together with deliberate care, then tugged him gently to the sectional, where the mirror across from it reflected everything. "You want to play judge and jury?" she whispered. "Good. You're about to witness your own conviction." She slowly turned him to face the mirror as she walked seductively behind him, rubbing her breast slowly alongside his arms that he had positioned at his waist. Standing behind him, she took her free hand and slowly started to undo the string at the top of his sweatpants. Then she slowly placed her hands inside his briefs, running her fingers down the crest of his pelvis.

"You've been a naughty boy, Counselor; who do you think you are making me wait," she said as she gently grabbed his now fully erect penis. She ran her hand down it and said seductively but assertively, "Now beg Your Honor for forgiveness." She began stroking his dick gently at a pace she knew would send him into moans. She had already added a small amount of lube to her hand to make the stroking more pleasurable for him.

"I'm sorry, Your Honor, my sincerest apologies," he said as he moaned out in pleasure, "Oooh shit."

She pushed him towards the door of the office. Once they reached the door, she stood behind him, continually stroking his dick until she felt the precum starting to drip out. She swirled it around on the tip of his dick before she let go.

She turned him around to face her and then pushed him down onto his knees in the middle of the room, arms tied in front of him, wrists bound, chest rising fast. "Tonight," she purred, "I'm the law, and your sorry is not good enough."

Aseeka stood over him and placed her left leg over his right shoulder, "Telling me you're sorry isn't enough; show me." She pushed her panties to the side and pushed her clit up against his forehead. Damon immediately lifted his head so his lips could meet her clit and slowly started to suck on it. He started out gently drawing it into his mouth while intensely rubbing his tongue over it. He could feel her getting wetter and wetter, and he knew she had been eating her pineapple from the sweet taste of her pussy juices that were now making their mark in his beard. He was great at eating pussy, sometimes too good, Aseeka thought as she felt her knees begin to slightly give in after a couple of minutes.

Damon was lost in her while also undoing the ties on his hands. Aseeka didn't notice because her head was leaned back as she moaned out in pleasure. Her pussy juices were now beginning to run down her leg.

"That's enough," she gasped out between her moans. But Damon ignored her because he was about to take control of the situation. He would stop when he was finished. He had undid the ties on his hands and put them on the floor while simultaneously pleasing her. He then slid his hands up the side of her hips and pushed her gently but intensely against the door. "

I'm about to cum," she screamed out. And just like that, he immediately stopped, put her leg on the ground, and stood over her. His 6'4" frame stared down at her 5'9" body.

"I think you must have forgotten how this works, Your Honor," he said, staring into her eyes intensely. You missed your last payment, and now I am forced to show your colleagues a revealing video of you in that vulnerable position. I'm sure they loved to see the judge face up ass down in the VIP private room of the strip club."

Her nipples were rock hard and piercing through her robe. He then took a nipple in each hand and squeezed them gently with his fingertips.

"No, please don't! I'll do anything," Asseka cried out as the roles of dominance switched. "Please, I've worked hard to get here and don't want to lose it all behind a stupid mistake. I was drunk and.."

He placed his index finger over her lips, "I don't give a fuck about that, now get on your knees and show me how sorry you are," he said through a devious smile as he grabbed the flogger out of her hand and dropped it on the floor. "Now take off that fucking robe because I'm in charge," he said as he took a step to admire her thick ass body while she slowly undressed. "And leave those heels on."

Aseeka slowly started to remove her robe, and she let it drop to the floor. There she was, standing in a red-laced bra with matching panties and heels, trying to look as scared as possible. Damon was standing there looking at her with a mischievous smile and a sense of admiration for her beauty. He walked over to the sectional, grabbed a throw pillow off of it, and then made his way back toward her. He placed the pillow down on the floor and looked her directly in the eyes.

He said sternly, "On your knees, Your Honor." He gently touched the top of her head and pushed her down into a position where her knees would go gently onto the pillow. He took the head of his dick and parted her lips.

Aseeka was one of the best at sucking dick, if not the best, and she knew it. Ready to make him squirm, she slowly pulled his pants down to his ankles and took his dick into her mouth. She began to suck it gently. She intensified her sucks every so often until she had fully his dick in her mouth. She enjoyed feeling the shaft of his dick going back and forth in her mouth. She loved giving him a sloppy moment of ecstasy and watching his eyes roll back as she looked up at him, enjoying her ability to give him head. His dick was now reaching the back of her deep ass throat. She kept this motion for about 5 minutes before she felt his big thick ass dick starting to pulsate. Damon placed one of his hands on her head and the other hand on the door as he felt his knees weaken.

He cried out, "I'm cummin!" and tried to pull his dick out.

But Aseeka was back in control, for the moment. She wanted him to explode in her mouth so she could taste his sweet cum. And he obliged. She felt his hot come shooting in her mouth as he took his hand off her head and now had both hands on the door, supporting his body weight. But she wasn't done. She kept going. Damon could get hard again; he never had a problem in that area. So she kept going with his limp dick in her mouth. It took a few minutes for him to get hard again, but he was there, and she knew the second nut would be fierce.

Damon was standing over Aseeka, amazed at her ability to control his dick. He slowly moved it from his mouth and knew he had to regain control of the situation. "Stand your ass up," he said, still trying his best to control his breath. Aseeka obliged and said nothing. He then positioned the door restraints that were hanging over it and grabbed her hands one by one, placing each of them in a restraint. He knew to do it tight enough to make her feel completely submissive, but they were always cautious just in case she needed to free herself for any reason.

Aseeka stared into Damon's dark brown eyes and waited for him to proceed. Her heartbeat was increasing rapidly. He took his foot and kicked both of her legs open. He placed his right hand around her neck and squeezed it just enough to bring her complete submission. She listened as he commanded, "Tell me who the fuck is in charge." She could smell his warm, minty breath against her face as he held on to her neck while pressing his nose against hers.

"You are; please don't hurt me," she begged.

He slowly released her neck and slid his hand down between her titties. Then to her belly button, all while he pressed his face against hers. Then he slowly slid his index finger and middle finger down between her pussy lips as he began to kiss her intensely. Placing his soft, wet, thick ass tongue in her mouth. He slid it out and smiled at her, flexing his pretty white teeth through his devious-ass smile. He was in full blackmail character now, just like she liked it. She felt him push his fingers inside of her wet ass pussy and slowly start to move them in and out. He knew exactly what she liked, as they had been in this scenario before. Damon wasn't like most men; he took the time to learn her body, and she took the time to understand his. He pushed his fingers directly to her G-spot and began pressing down on it.

"Oh, stop, ple—" She attempted to moan as she felt herself about to cum; he pulled his fingers out.

"You're not allowed to cum," he said matter-of-factly, his lips brushing against hers. Until I say, you can."

He walked over to the flogger, bent over, and grabbed it off the floor by the braided leather handle. He walked over to Aseeka and turned her around swiftly. He had lowered the restraints just enough to make them adjustable so she could do a 180-degree turn. He then took his foot and kicked her legs open again. He pushed the middle of her back so that her ass would perk out just enough. Aseeka didn't have a fat juicy ass like the girls in the music videos, but she had enough to make it clap. She called it bedroom booty. They often jokingly referred to it as her BRB because it wasn't big enough to be a BBL. Damon took the flogger and ran it down her back until he reached the small of her back. He then let it fall between her ass cheeks, where he moved it up and down slowly.

He whispered in her ear, "What's your pain threshold today?"

She replied submissively, "A seven."

He then took a step back to create enough room between him and her protruding ass cheeks. He bent his arm in a position to release the flogger and smacked her directly on the left ass cheek and then the right.

Aseeka moaned loudly, "Ohhh." Damon repeated the same act four more times, just enough to see her ass cheeks beginning to turn red. He stopped and smacked one with his free hand. He then dropped the flogger to the ground as he walked back closely to her. He took his right hand and slid his fingers underneath her ass cheeks to her pussy hole and started to rub her clit from the back.

He whispered in her ear while fingering her, "You ready for me to fuck your brains out? I bet you'll pay your fee on time moving forward, won't you?"

"Yes, please, let me go. I have the money in the drawer. I can pay you now," she cried out.

"Nah, you can pay me later, but first, that pussy going pay as interest," he laughed loudly.

She felt the head of Damon's dick parting her pussy hole as he shoved it into her tight throbbing pussy and began fucking her with ruthless vigor. The sounds of his pelvis smacking against her ass could be heard at the front door. He paused and released her from the restraints. He was mindful of not having her hands in an upward position for too long. And he knew she was about to be in for a long night. Once he released her from the restraints, he momentarily pulled his dick out and told her to walk over to the desk and told her to bend over it.

Aseeka complied and felt him lift her right leg up on the desk to position it so that he had full access to her pussy. He placed his dick right back in her pussy hole and began thrusting out at an even more intense pace. He could tell that she had been doing her Kegels. He enjoyed feeling the tightness of her pussy walls gripping his dick, and her loud moans were turning him on even more. He started sporadically smacking her ass as he fucked her. He paused for a second, and with his dick still inside of her, he took his thumb and wet it with the juices leaking out of her pussy and started making a small circle around her ass hole.

Aseeka knew what he was about to do; at first, when he would stick his finger in her ass, she didn't know what to think, but now she liked it. In fact, she loved it! As the thoughts were racing through her head, she felt the pressure from his thumb enter her ass hole. He pressed it in and out and then slowly began doing the same thing with her dick in her pussy hole. She felt her body heating up even more, her pussy throbbing; she knew she was about to cum! She was now moaning loudly and uncontrollably. The sensation of having multiple holes in her body led her into a climactic state about a minute later.

"Oh my God," she hollered out as she felt the cum shooting out of her body. And she collapsed over the desk, but knew they weren't done. Damon flipped her over immediately; his firm ass knew precisely how to manhandle her when she allowed him to.

He smiled. "You're not allowed to cum," he said matter-of-factly, lips brushing hers. "Not until I say so. "That'll cost you a punishment."

Staring deeply into her eyes, he grabbed her by the throat and said controllably, "I'm going to go sit in that chair over there, and you are going to ride my dick until I tell you to stop.

He walked around the left side of the desk and sat in her office chair like a king taking his throne. Aseeka pulled herself together and followed him. She slowly threw her right leg over his lap to face him. She then kissed him in the mouth for a good 5 seconds before she grabbed his dick and strategically placed herself on his lap. He was right; she had been working on her Kegels, and she was about to show him the results of her pussy routine. Straddling him in slow, calculated motion, her warm body pressing against his skin, she slowly started to bounce up and down on his dick, intentionally letting her titties bounce in his face. She placed her right hand around the front of his thick ass neck. She was about to take back control. The sounds of his moans were turning her on, and she knew choking Damon would only send him into a pleasurable frenzy.

She said confidently, "You're not so tough now, are you? Feel that tight wet pussy on your big ass dick." She started to bounce more as she tightened her pussy by flexing her pelvic muscles. Damon was lost in her, moaning loudly and trying to muddle the word, stop. But she ignored him and just kept bouncing. She could feel his dick beginning to pulsate inside of her.

"Come on, Counselor, state your case while I give you this pussy" she said. Damon placed his hands on her ass cheeks and squeezed to let her know he was about to cum.

"I'm cummin!," he said in a bit of a high-pitched voice that made her giggle.

"Not yet." She just stared into his eyes as she *rolled* her hips once, slow and intentional, feeling every inch of him press up into her heat.

She immediately jumped off and bent down at his feet and started taking his pulsating dick in her mouth, moving up and down slowly. Damon was now moaning loudly. Just as she felt his cum shooting out of his urethra, she pulled his dick out and lathered her face with his cum. His body had jerked throughout the explosion, and he collapsed entirely in the chair. Aseeka stood up and grabbed a pack of body wipes from the top drawer of her desk. She wiped her face off first and then gently cleaned off the remaining semen, combined with her pussy juices, from Damon's lap as he was still unable to move and trying his best to regain his composure.

"I'll grab a bucket of ice and some champagne. Meet me by the fireplace," she said, kissed him gently, then walked over to grab his T-shirt off the floor and put it on. It was just long enough to drop past her thighs. She looked over her left shoulder right before she walked out the door and said, "Don't make me wait too long, or I might have to come back up here."

"Whatever, your Honor," Damon responded as he finally regained his composure and could sit up straight. "I'll be down in a second. You got any D'USSÉ? I'm not feeling champagne."

"You know I do," she yelled back as she made her way down to the bar in the living room. "I'll have it ready for you on ice boo."

He cursed under his breath, "Fuck, that shit was good."

Damon was lying on his side facing Aseeka, who was lying on her side facing him, her back to the fireplace. He admired how the light from the fire radiated off her beautiful skin. He knew her body all too well and also knew her. He could see that something was on her mind, even though she tried to play it off.

He said empathetically, "What's up, babe? Something is on your mind; you've been quieter than normal."

"I'll tell you when the time is right, it's just work shit, some stuff with an upcoming case I need to process before I say it out loud." But truthfully, she didn't know if she could tell him the whole story. It was a secret she had long buried. One she'd sworn she'd take to the grave with her.

"When we speak, we are afraid our words will not be heard or welcomed, but when we are silent, we are still afraid, so it is better to speak," he said as he smiled through his pearly white teeth.

"Ok then, Audre Lorde, " she said, laughing but admiring his artistic recount of the famous poem.

"We've been doing this for a long time, and I know you well enough not to push you to tell me. I know you well enough to see that it's troubling you, whatever it is. As a people, we must improve at expressing ourselves and knowing when to lean on one another in times of trouble. Whether it's mental, physical, or spiritual discomfort, remember it's ok to share your burden, babe, he said. I teach my sons not to hold onto what bothers them and to use their words to communicate their challenges. Sometimes, when you're ready, the best way to share is to begin saying whatever it is out loud."

Aseeka felt ashamed as she quickly decided not to share everything, which bothered her because she hadn't yet had time to process it. "This case came across my desk today, and I know the offender. I haven't seen this person in decades, and I only knew them formally, but we're familiar."

"Do you need to hand the case over to someone? I'm happy to take it if you don't feel comfortable, he said in a supportive tone."

The thought had crossed her mind as she responded, "I don't know yet, but when you decide what to do with it, I promise you'll be the first to know. "

He nodded as he sipped his D'USSÉ on the rocks. The glass pressed against his beautiful, thick lips, and he stared at her with sincerity and concern, "It's bothering you, huh? I'm here if you need to talk. I know you have a case with that doctor who mishandled some female patients. It originally came through my desk, but I couldn't look too deep into it; the defendant was my wife's uncle. I had to hand it off due to a conflict of interest."

Aseeka felt her heart sink into her stomach; she felt a hard knot develop in her throat. "Yeah, I saw the case file today; I didn't know that came from you; I haven't even read it thoroughly yet. She knew she wasn't wholly truthful but wasn't ready to explain, especially after she found out Damon knew him.

"Yeah, I never really got to meet that side of her family; Gillian used to say that side had issues. Her parents would call them generationally cursed. They got into all kinds of ugly mess, so we stayed away from them," he said proudly.

Aseeka could barely make the words come out of her mouth; she felt like she would throw up. But she swallowed hard and regained herself once she heard his ringer go off on his phone.

He picked it up, swiped to answer it, and then put it on speaker. Aseeka saw the name of his son go on the screen. "What's up, baby boy?" he said as he answered. Aseeka was grateful for the interruption. His oldest twin, Damian, came out two minutes earlier than his brother Donovan.

"We're almost ready; we should be out of practice in the next 45 minutes. Are you going to meet us at home or the theatre?" his son asked enthusiastically.

Damon almost forgot about Friday's movie night. It was the first Friday of every month, and he and his sons would see the newest horror or action flick together. It was one of his favorite things to do! Aseeka had met his sons and loved how he instilled respect and discipline in them, and she also loved how much he loved his kids.

"I'll meet y'all at the theatre; the last show starts at 10 p.m., right? Wait, did y'all finish y'all's homework?"

They would see the newest Jordan Peele flick about a woman haunting a family. The boys were excited about its release, which was opening night. Damon was excited that he could reserve tickets and invited Aseeka while they were at work earlier that day, but she declined.

"Yes, Dad, we always finish our homework," said Damian.

You could hear Donovan in the back yelling, "Come on now, old man, you know how we do, we roll on the honor roll. The ladies don't like the dummies."

"Speaking of ladies, where are you? Aseeka's house?" said Damian teasingly.

Damon reminded him, "Yes, and you're on speakerphone, so watch it!"

"Heeeyyy, Aseeka," they both said in unison.

She laughed and replied, "Hey, fellas, how are y'all?" She never really hung out with him and his sons, but she would see them when she dropped by the house or spent the night over at Damon's. They were always respectful, but she never felt comfortable going out with them on family nights. She and Damon had yet to become official, and even though the boys didn't seem to mind, she didn't feel ready. She knew they were still in therapy, dealing with the grief of losing their mother, and she wanted to respect their boundaries. However, she often wondered if she could successfully play the step-mommy role. She and Damon started messing around about a year after his wife's passing. They started to become consistently involved after about three years of doing whatever in the fuck they were doing. They never placed a label on it, and she was OK with that for now. They had talked about being an item before, but Damon wasn't ready to label it, and she didn't question it because she liked her freedom. She wasn't out there fucking anybody else, but she did like her freedom. However, they secretly pondered when to touch on being in a monogamous relationship again.

"We're good, and how are you?" they said.

"I'm great, thanks for asking," she replied

Damon took over the conversation, "I'll meet y'all at the theatre in 30 min. This one is on y'all, right?"

Donavon shouted, "How are we going to pay for it with our good looks?"

Damian said, "If we relied on your good looks, we'd never get anywhere!"

"You look just like me, fool! We are identical!" Donavon fired back.

Everyone erupted in laughter.

Damon said through laughter, "Alright, I'll see y'all in a second."

He hung up and looked at Aseeka, "You know you're welcome to come."

"Yeah, but I'm tired, and I'm not that into horror flicks," she stated as she yawned.

Damon smiled at her, "Yeah, I did wear that shit out. But it's Friday night, so call your friends. You had a long week, so get out and do something. Let ya hair down, babe!"

Aseeka looked him in the eye, "First of all, I did my thing, too, screamer, and I already had happy hour with the crew before you arrived. Tasha, Chanel, and I will attend Malik's and Syd's concert in the park tomorrow. You should drop by and say hi."

He started to get up off the floor, "Nope, I can't. We're having dinner with my mother and father for my dad's birthday tomorrow. Malik and Syd's crowd isn't my scene; he and the Gwerls are a little too ratchet for me. But hit me afterwards."

She lifted her arm, gesturing for him to help her up. He quickly obliged and pulled her up off the floor. She took off his shirt and stood there naked as she helped him put it back on. "Ok, I will," she said as she smirked, watching him lick his lips and admire her from head to toe.

"You know what the fuck you be doing," Damon said as he followed her to the door smacking her on the ass. She opened the door and watched him put on his size-11 Adidas Men's Yeezy Foam Runner GX4472 Stone Sages. He kissed her passionately on the lips as he came up cuffing her butt cheek with both hands.

"I'll hit you later," he said as he came up for air.

She smiled, "Text me when y'all get home safe."

He nodded as he turned to walk down the hall.

She closed the door swiftly and walked to the bathroom. She did a once-over in the mirror and decided to take a bath.

The bathtub was less a fixture and more a freestanding, deep shrine made of smooth black volcanic stone that absorbed heat like it had a secret to keep. It sat in the center of her spa-like suite, perfectly positioned beneath a frosted skylight that bathed the room in diffused moonlight. The floor was warm to the touch, radiant with soft heat, and the walls were tiled in a matte charcoal that whispered calm.

She moved through the space like a ritual, barefoot, bare-shouldered, wrapped in nothing but the steam of her hot bath that was beginning to rise. With a slow twist of her wrist, she turned the brushed gold faucet knob higher, and water gushed out in a soft cascade, warm and whispering. As the tub began filling, she grabbed the pack of her Dr. Teal's Eucalyptus scented bath salt and bubble bath on the shelf above the tub. She poured them into the water. A few drops of ylang-ylang oil and a sliver of amber soap left her skin smelling like fire and luxury.

The water turned a smoky blush from the salts, and the scent lifted into the air, soft, floral, and grounding. She lit a single red candle and set it on the tub's edge, its flame catching in the reflection of the full-length mirror opposite her. She then walked over and twisted the knob on the wall to completely turn down the lights. She loved to set the mood, even when she was alone.

She didn't rush.

She walked back to the tub and stepped in slowly, letting the water climb up her calves, thighs, and hips, sinking into it like a queen returning to her throne. The tub embraced her, the heat curling around her muscles, dissolving the weight of the courtroom, the headlines, and the silence of her penthouse when the door closed behind her.

She leaned back, a soft sigh slipping from her lips, and let the water cover her chest, the flogger, the robe, the armor of the day, gone. In the bath, Aseeka Sinclair wasn't the judge. She was just a woman. Beautiful. Tired. Deserving.

And not to be disturbed.

She didn't want to think about the upcoming case, especially after the bomb Damon dropped on her about the doctor whose case she was presiding over. She would worry about it in the morning. But she would focus on her wellness for the rest of the night. She sipped her champagne and called, "Alexa, play my Sade playlist."

And with that, she relaxed and drifted into a meditative state—no more anxious thoughts. Or so she thought.

Chapter 5: Ghosts in the Chamber

The morning light crept through the blinds like an unwelcome guest.

Aseeka sat at her desk, the file for **People vs. Dr. Leonard Garvin** opened before her. She hadn't even touched her coffee. Her fingers hovered over the first page, then pulled back like the paper might burn her.

She knew every word in that file already because she'd read it thrice after Damon left. She couldn't sleep after bathing, so she got out of bed after staring at the ceiling for two hours, racing thoughts, and grabbed the case file from her work bag. As she took the file out of her bag, the black envelope from Byron dropped on the floor. She paused and picked it up. She admired the softness of the envelope and took a second to open it, trying her best not to compromise its beauty. She grabbed a letter opener and sliced it open. Immediately, she noticed there was a gold ticket inside the sleek envelope. She picked it up and noticed there was a QR code on it. It had the word *WELCOME* sitting about an inch above the code. She grabbed her phone and scanned the code, which took her to a portal website. *You must be 18 and over to enter; if so, click here,* she read as she clicked the link. And what she saw next intrigued her. It was the scene of one of Byron's little freak fests. She recalled how half-naked and naked people of all shapes and sizes in masquerade masks were on a well-lit dance floor. Strippers danced on a stage on a pole, and people danced seductively inside cages. The floor was entirely made of glass, and the camera panned down to show a full-fledged adult orgy happening on the bottom floor. She immediately felt intrigued. The scene on the screen shifted entirely to the orgy. A man was behind a woman fucking her doggy style while her mouth was wide open. Aseeka noticed another naked woman lying on her back directly in a 69-position underneath her with her head between her legs, devouring the other woman's pussy, who was being fucked in the doggy style position, as she moaned loudly. The camera panned directly to her wide-open mouth and zoomed into her tonsils. The special effects were terrific and seductive, Aseeka thought to herself. And then a sign flashed across the screen saying to click here to reserve your spot for the grand opening in Los Angeles.

Aseeka paused for a minute and thought, am I going to do this, as she remembered the smirk on Byron's face. He had worked hard to get some of his former teammates to become investors in his venture. She knew it would be lit, and she did want to experience it, even if it was just once. She preferred to do it in LA rather than in Chicago because nobody would know her there.

Tasha had been trying to get her to go for the longest. And she could hear Tasha in her head saying, "Girl, come the fuck on! Sign the NDA, and let's be on our way." Alright, fine, she thought as she clicked on the sign. Immediately, an NDA popped up, which she read carefully. It was pretty legit, and she appreciated the professionalism in writing it. She knew Byron was a serious businessman, but damn. She clicked the sign and was redirected to a page where her information had already been filled in the prompt. This man, Byron, had personalized the invites using a coding system. Below the prompt, it had the option to click, *attending, maybe, or not attending.* She felt a bit of anxiety as she clicked *attending.* There was no turning back now, she thought to herself. She was all in and would tell Tasha the good news on their way to Malik and Syd's performance.

"Ok, let me get my ass back to work," she said out loud as she turned her attention back to the brief.

The first words she saw stood out loudly as she read the charges.

Sexual misconduct.
Assault.
Abuse of power.

The details were clinical procedural. But behind every line, she saw herself, 23, fresh out of law school, trying to navigate a world built to swallow her whole. She had just passed the bar and was ready to take on the world!

She could still feel the cold of that exam room, the weight of his hand on her thigh, and how he smiled at her afterward like nothing had happened. She never told anyone. Not her friends. Not her family. Not even Dr. Bruno, and he'd been dragging her therapy ass for years.

Back then, she couldn't afford to be weak. Or what she presumed to be weak, as she was learning that even her understanding of that was a misconception. Over time, she discovered strength in speaking up and owning your authenticity. Back then, she didn't have the mindset or the words. She'd already been the girl with a father in prison, the scholarship kid in rooms where people who didn't look like her felt she wasn't supposed to be in. At that time, weakness would've swallowed her whole.

Now he was back, not as a ghost but as a defendant.

Aseeka flipped to the witness list, and her stomach flipped with it as she reviewed the history of his case file.

One name stood out: David McGregor.

Her father. His full name was David Sinclair McGregor. Her father had murdered Galvin's brother back in the day!

Her heart slammed against her ribs.

She flipped through the supplemental file, her eyes scanning, her breath catching when she read:

The defendant's brother, Marcus Voss, is deceased. Homicide. Convicted murderer: David McGregor-Sinclair.

Her mouth went dry.

Her father hadn't told her this. She knew he killed a man, but she figured it was over her street dealings. This wasn't in any family conversation. And now, she was presiding over a case where the victim's brother had died at her father's hands.

Her head fell into her hands.

What the hell was she supposed to do now?

Chapter 6: The Gynecologist

Aseeka had pulled up to the doctor's office, ready to deal with the discomfort of having her annual Pap smear and mammogram. The gynecologist, Dr. Garvin, had come highly recommended by her mother. Her mother had just switched into her new role, Dr. Monica Sinclair, as the School Principal of Malcolm X Elementary School about six months ago. The job came with better benefits, plus a substantial pay raise that was enough to move them to a better neighborhood. When she switched her role, since they had moved into a new school district, she changed her insurance, allowing her children to stay enrolled until they were 26. Thankfully, Aseeka had insurance through her job, and she was happy that she was in her provider area, so she didn't need her mother's plan. She liked her independence.

Their mother was very intentional about taking them to the doctor for annual check-ups as children, especially since sickle cell anemia had run in her father's side of the family. She wanted to ensure her children and herself were healthy and didn't have the gene. Luckily, her children took after her side of the family, but that didn't stop them from possibly inheriting the bad health that troubled many Black families. High cholesterol, diabetes, and high blood pressure were all things her mother remained conscious of as she tried her best to keep her and her children healthy and not allow them to become another statistic.

Aseeka kept her annual check-ups and stayed active, running track and field and playing volleyball throughout her life. She was always a heavier-set girl, ranging from 180 to 190 lbs. in school, and at 5'9", she carried it well. When she graduated from high school, she received a full-ride scholarship to Northwestern, where she majored in criminal justice in undergrad and graduate school. She was on her way to pursue a juris doctorate at Georgetown University, where she also earned a full ride. She was active in community work in high school because she was raised by her mother, an educational activist fighting the institutional education-to-prison pipeline. Her grandmother, Cassie McGregor, was a community activist who loved to host neighborhood block parties and worked with the Blank Panther party to set up healthcare clinics in poor black neighborhoods in Harlem in the 1960s. So, personal and community health had always been a priority for her family.

She had just turned 23 and was ready to take on her new challenges, but first, she had to ensure she was healthy. She had been sexually active since 20, and she was pretty open with her mother about it since her mother was big on sex education and started her teaching career as a sex-ed educator. They talked often about birth control, safe sex practices, and more about STIs than she would have liked, but she appreciated her mother's openness and willingness to be a safe space. Her mother preferred abstinence, but always created a space for her children to talk to her about their sexuality. And she encouraged them to stay adamant about their health. So she was happy to refer her daughter to Dr. Garvin. So she called. Made the appointment. Showed up.

As she pulled up to the doctor's office, blasting "Magic Stick" by Lil Kim, she was mentally preparing for a new doctor to examine her coochie. Her mother had gone to him earlier and raved about how pleasant he was during her exams. Aseeka's natural kinky hair, freshly waxed and shaven, was pulled up in a top-knot ponytail.. She wasn't about to meet Dr. Garvin with a hair coochie and hairy legs and have this doctor calling her she-wolf behind her back. She liked to keep her body tidy. She wore a white Michael Jordan summer dress with the Air Jordan logo in the center of the chest and White and red Jordan sandals. Being from the Chi, they were big Jordan fans! Her older brother, Anthony, worked at the Nike store and had the hookup on all the latest Jordan gear. So she stayed fitted.

After graduating with her BA in criminal justice, she worked as a law clerk at the small private law firm of Finker and Associates, a Black-owned firm.. She knew the team there well because she interned as an undergrad and then received an offer for a job as a clerk after completing her master's degree because of her hard work. She was a high performer and proud of it, and she never let anything stop her from pursuing her goals.

She was happy to see a parking space near the front door that said: "Reserved for Garvin Clinic Patients Only." She pulled into the parking space and turned down her music. It was a cold fall day in Chicago, and she had her windows down, enjoying the crisp air hitting her skin as she drove 10 minutes from her apartment to the doctor's office. She planned to meet the Gwerls for lunch after her noon appointment.

Dr. Leonard Garvin's medical office sat tucked between a smoothie bar and a tax service in a South Side Chicago strip mall, its unassuming brick exterior doing little to prepare visitors for the carefully curated space inside. The waiting room was clean and well-kept, if not a little too sterile beneath the surface, like it was trying a bit too hard to say "Welcome," helping patients to overcome any discomfort.

When she walked into the office, she could smell the ocean breeze, Glade Plug-ins filling the air. A bold mural dominated one wall, grabbed her attention, a vibrant painting of a Black family standing in front of a modest home, their faces radiant with hope and generational strength. The family was painted in sunset tones: the father holding a toddler, the mother pregnant and glowing, and the children playing in the background as if joy was their birthright. She smiled, for real. It reminded her of home. Of what Black care is supposed to feel like.

The front desk was a whole scene. Miss Loretta, regal in a purple cardigan, looked up from her monitor, eyes sharp behind her glasses. "ID and insurance card, baby," she said in that church-lady voice that makes you sit up straighter. Behind her, Kaylie popped her gum and waved, her fingers clicking against her phone screen. Cornrows tight to her scalp, nails long and neon pink. "Hey boo!" she chirped, not even looking up. The front desk was tidy and functional along the left side of the lobby. Behind it sat the two very different women who somehow managed to keep the office running like clockwork.

Aseeka laughed under her breath, shaking her head. It's chaotic. But it was familiar. It felt safe.

She signed in and sat, flipping through a worn *Essence* magazine with Destiny's Child on the cover. A flyer caught her eye: free prenatal yoga at the Y. Another poster shows a smiling Black woman with the words "Know Your Numbers: High Blood Pressure Kills." Everything is tailored for women like her. Young. Black. Vulnerable. Seen.

On the coffee table in front of her, a stack of neatly arranged magazines offered outdated issues of *Essence*, *Parents,* and *Jet*, all fanned out beneath a jar of peppermints. Laminated community health flyers lined the adjacent wall as posters about breast cancer awareness, infant nutrition, hypertension in Black men, and free prenatal classes.

The office tried to present itself as warm and trustworthy, a safe place for Black families, especially women. But beneath the posters, the mural, and behind Dr. Garvin's framed credentials hung in the hallway. Within minutes, a nurse with a chart in hand walked through the door, scanned the waiting room as if it were filled with other people, and said, "Aseeka Sinclair."

Aseeka jumped up, to herself, "Damn, that was quick." She followed the nurse past that mural into a softly lit exam room with light jazz playing overhead. The nurse asked her to step on a scale and recorded her weight at 176 lbs. and height at 5'10". She was an inch taller and didn't tell Aseeka to remove her sandals. The nurse then asked her to sit as she took her blood pressure. Aseeka tried to sit as still as possible as the nurse wrapped the plugged cuff around the sphygmomanometer, which squeezed her right arm. The nurse smiled once she read the final results on the screen and was happy to tell her that it was normal. The nurse was sweet. Mid-30s, maybe, with knotless braids pulled into a loose bun and a smile that reminded Aseeka of her cousin from the West Side. She held a tablet and a gentle authority that made you want to sit up straighter without being told.

"Go ahead and have a seat, Miss Sinclair," she said, motioning toward the exam table covered in fresh paper. "Dr. Garvin will be with you in just a few."

Aseeka settled onto the crinkling paper, her purse clutched in her lap. She hated doctors' offices. The artificial cold, the quiet buzz of fluorescent lights, the way everything smelled faintly of lemon and something sterile. But the ocean breeze was helping to mask the smell of medical institutions. But this place felt ... different. Softer.

"Alright, just a few questions for intake," the nurse said, tapping her screen with long, lavender nails. "Full name?"

"Aseeka Marie Sinclair," she replied, her voice a little too formal.

"Date of birth?"

"April 20th."

The nurse paused and raised a brow. "Mmm. Taurus. That tracks."

Aseeka chuckled just a little, the tension in her shoulders loosening.

"Any medication allergies?"

"Penicillin."

"Got it. Taking any prescriptions or supplements right now?"

"Just a multivitamin and iron. I was a little anemic last year."

The nurse nodded, clearly unfazed. "Common, especially for us. Last menstrual cycle?"

"About two weeks ago. Regular."

"Any pain, irregularities, anything like that?"

"Some cramps, but nothing major. Pretty standard."

The nurse tapped notes in with quick ease, barely looking down.

"And are you sexually active?"

Aseeka hesitated. Just for a second. "Yes."

"Birth control?"

"Condoms," she said. "No hormones."

"Gotcha. Any specific concerns or symptoms today?"

"No ... just a general check-up. Haven't been in a while."

The nurse smiled and gave a soft, affirming nod. "Alright. Well, you're in good hands. Dr. Garvin is the best. He's gentle and knows what he's doing. Just let him know if you have questions or need anything during the visit." The nurse reached into a drawer and pulled out a gown. "Please undress, remove everything, even your underwear, for the pap smear and the breast exam. The doctor should arrive shortly. We're not too busy today."

She gave Aseeka a reassuring look, then slipped out the door with practiced quiet, leaving her alone in the stillness.

Aseeka looked around the room. Then quickly undressed, folding her clothes and placing them and her purse on a chair in the corner of the room. She climbed onto the patient table, leaving her sandals beside the table, and just observed the room while she waited. Her eyes lingered on a laminated poster showing the reproductive system in pastel colors and a plastic model of a uterus on a dusty tray beside the sink. The soft hum of the overhead lights filled the silence. She crossed her ankles. Smoothed her skirt. The paper beneath her thighs crackled as she adjusted her posture, the room more marvelous than expected. Aseeka wore the thin cotton gown they gave her, open in the front, just like the nurse instructed. Her arms were folded over her chest, fingers gripping her elbows like she could anchor herself with her body.

Everything had felt normal.

Safe.

Until it didn't.

After about 10 minutes, she heard a knock on the door. "Come in," she said jokingly.

Dr. Garvin enters like he's known her forever. Kind smile. Soft voice. Expensive cologne. He was about 5'9" and looked like a dark-skinned Rick Fox, she thought. He was cute and built like he had a regular gym routine. He was thick, like a college running back, and his voice was soft, deep, and welcoming.

"Hey there, Miss Sinclair. How are we feeling today?"

He smiled when he walked in, chart in hand, closing the door behind him gently, like he was sealing off the world. He wore a charcoal button-down under his white coat, a stethoscope draped around his neck like a decoration. His energy was calm. Reassuring. Polished.

"I'm good," Aseeka replied a little too quickly.

"Good. Let's keep it that way."

He flipped through her chart, then gave her that familiar smile that disarmed people. "Alright, we'll do a basic physical today and a routine breast exam. Nothing major, just making sure everything's in working order."

He complimented her name, asked what law school she was attending, and said she would be his lawyer one day. Or even a great judge. She liked him already.

A little flattered and nervous, she laughs, "I just graduated with my master's from Northwestern, and I'm headed to Georgetown!"

"Ooh, a soon-to-be Hoya, very nice, I prefer Maroons!" he said jokingly.

Aseeka laughed, "Not the University of Chicago … and I was just starting to like you!"

He smiled again and began to talk to her through the procedure, explaining what he would do step by step. He then asked her to lie back on the table. As she lay back, there was a knock at the door.

"Enter," he said in a calm and commanding voice.

Ms. Loretta said, "Hey, we're headed to lunch, and I will lock the waiting room door. They usually locked the door when they headed to lunch because they had an incident before where someone walked in and walked out with a laptop.

"I have your order, and I'll text you if anything changes."

"Ok, thank you," he said without missing a beat. And waited for her to close the door before he continued.

He then told her he was going to examine her breast first. So he pulled down her gown until about six inches below her breast, completely exposing them. He told her to lift up both her arms and keep them over her head.

He warmed his hands by rubbing them together, a gesture meant to be considerate. "Hands might be a little cold, but I'll be gentle."

And he was, at first.

He started with clinical precision. Pressing along the outer edges of her left breast with the flat pads of his fingers. Circular motion. Light pressure. She tried to focus on the ceiling. On her breathing.

But then ... something shifted.

His touch slowed. Grew more deliberate. His fingers lingered longer in the spaces between. He exhaled softly. Close. Too close. And when his knuckles grazed the underside of her breast, his voice dropped.

"You've got perfect tissue elasticity. Most women your age don't notice these things, but your body ..." He trailed off like he caught himself, only he didn't stop. He looked at her, not clinically, but curiously. Intimately.

She told herself not to move. Not to flinch. Maybe she was misreading it. Maybe this was normal. Maybe doctors said weird shit sometimes.

But when he moved to her other breast, the contact wasn't just medical. His palm flattened, covering her more than necessary. His thumb traced a line no one had asked for. His breathing changed. So did hers.

She looked away. She focused on the mural in her mind. The waiting room. The receptionist with the gum. The peppermint jar. Anything but the growing realization that this was not what care felt like.

She wanted to speak. But her throat tightened.

He smiled again, like nothing had happened. "Everything looks good. Let's move to the next phase, your pap smear. She did so, all the while her mind racing. She was thinking to herself, should I even let him down there? But it was all happening so quickly. He had her legs spread open, and she couldn't do anything about it.

The paper on the exam table rustled beneath her as she scooted down as the doctor instructed. "Feet in the stirrups, drape over your lap, and just try to relax," he said. Easy for him to say. Aseeka lay back, eyes fixed on the ceiling tiles as her knees parted and the cold metal of the footrests cradled her calves. The room was too quiet. The air is too cold. Her gown was open beneath the paper sheet, her body exposed in ways that made her skin crawl, even though she hadn't yet figured out why. To her surprise, she started to feel turned on. She thought to herself, "What the fuck is happening? Am I tripping? Why is my body responding like this?

Dr. Garvin spoke, and his tone was smooth and professional.

"Alright, Miss Sinclair, let's get your Pap done and out of the way. You're doing great."

He donned gloves slowly, deliberately, like a ritual he'd done a thousand times. She tried not to watch. She focused on the community health poster with the smiling Black mother and baby on the wall across from her. It felt a bit awkward now.

"This might feel a little cold," he said softly as he sat between her legs. His chair rolled forward. Her breath caught. She felt frozen, helpless, and, for some reason, a slight sense of intrigue.

He opened her with the speculum, cool, metallic, mechanical. She flinched. Not because of the pain but because of how his touch felt so … intentional. Like he was watching her reaction, studying it.

"There we go," he murmured, a voice dipped lower than necessary. "Your cervix looks … perfect."

Her brows knit together. Was that normal? Did doctors say that?

His gloved fingers moved next. Not the sterile, swift swab she expected. He moved slowly, like he was reading her body instead of examining it. Like he was savoring something no one had offered him. Like he was admiring her pussy!

A shiver ran down her spine. She felt the swab enter her as he collected routine samples for the lab. She felt a bit ashamed because she could feel her vagina getting wetter. So she tensed up.

"Relax for me," he said. "Let me know if anything feels uncomfortable."

It was uncomfortable. But not in the way the pamphlets warned about. It was the kind of discomfort that creeps under your skin and whispers you're not safe, but not loud enough to scream over the silence.

She felt frozen. Trapped in a body that refused to betray her thoughts.

"Ok, good," he said as he placed the swab in a tube and swiftly removed the speculum. "We have just one more procedure, and then we'll be done. Please try to relax. Do you always naturally lubricate like this during an exam?"

Oh my God, she thought in embarrassment, as her emotions must've run over her face.

"It's genuinely okay. I'm a gynecologist and trust me, I have seen everything," he said.

Aseeka was too embarrassed to respond; she lay there frozen with shame.

He was now standing between her legs, staring directly at her. She hadn't noticed that he had removed his gloves. And then, just as suddenly, she felt his two fingers enter her wet pussy, and he took his free hand and pressed down on her lower abdomen right above her pelvic region as if he was conducting a formal exam.

"I'm just checking for any irregularities," he stated as he shoved his fingers in and out of her. She was trying her best not to moan as she felt the pleasure from his fingers rubbing against her pussy walls. Her mind was racing, asking all sorts of questions. What the fuck kind of exam is this? And suddenly, he found what he was looking for, her G-spot. He began pressing his fingers against it, and Aseeka was now quietly moaning. She wanted to tell him to stop; she knew it was wrong, but she couldn't. She was so embarrassed that she was feeling pleasure, and no man had yet to hit her G-spot. She didn't even think she had one! Her body started to jerk as he kept going, and she could feel her insides heating up. You could hear his fingers thrusting in and out of her as the sound of her wet pussy made a gushing sound.

He took his hand off her abdomen and began rubbing her clitoris with his free hand. Aseeka felt her back arch; she was too scared to tell him to stop. She didn't know if she did or didn't want him to quit as the rubbing became more intense and her body grew warmer and warmer. And just like that, she erupted, gripping the paper underneath her body. And before she could do anything, she saw him sit back down in the chair and felt his tongue grazing against her protruding clit. He was sopping up her cum and used his hands to spread her thighs as he kept her legs propped open on the stirrups. She could hear him sucking on her clit, and she could feel his lips and his tongue moving in a slow circular motion creating a sense of pleasure she had never felt before.

"Wait, please," she said as she lay back, unable to move. She didn't know if she was paralyzed with fear or pleasure.

"Almost done," he muttered as he spoke directly into her pussy. And just like that, she felt herself cum again. This time was more intense than the first as she felt her body jerk intensely, and she squirted for the first time ever in her doctor's face!

He quickly stood up, grabbed a paper towel, cleaned off his face, and then grabbed a wet wipe off the tray and cleaned up Aseeka. I'll send the nurse in to collect your samples for the lab, and you should have your results back in less than a week. I'll give you a few minutes to get yourself together."

And just like that, it was over. He withdrew, removed his gloves, and discarded them with a calm efficiency that made her question herself.

"You're all set," he said with a smile. "Textbook healthy. You've got nothing to worry about." And then he grabbed the clipboard off the tray and exited the office quickly.

But she did have something to worry about.

She worried about why her stomach turned, and the scent of lemon disinfectant nauseated her. Why did she feel like crying in the parking lot afterward and have no words to explain it?

She got up and put her clothes on in silence, confused. Ashamed. And not yet ready to call what happened what it was. But she had to tell someone. So she called Malik, her best friend, and he answered.

She sat frozen with the phone in her hand, "Malik, can I come over? I need to talk."

Malik: Yes, come through, girl. Are you good? You sound weird.

"I'll be there in a few. Have the Malbec ready for me," she said, still in a daze. Still not knowing if she would have the courage to say it out loud.

But now, years later, she could say it.

He violated me. While calling it care.

And then he left.

Just like that.

Leaving her in silence, the gown still open, her body humming with confusion, shame, and something she couldn't name at the time.

It lingered.

Something in her stomach knotted.

As she left, something clung to her. A feeling she couldn't name. There was a heat between her shoulder blades. Shame. Confusion. Pleasure. Not realizing that she could feel those things simultaneously, her mother, the sex educator, had never explained this to her!

And now, years later, sitting in chambers staring at his name on a court docket, it hit her like a wave.

It wasn't just a check-up.

Chapter 7: Bruno's Warning

Dr. Bruno sat in his usual royal blue leather chair, legs crossed, notepad in his lap, glasses resting on the edge of his nose like always. The scent of sage and cedar lingered from the diffuser in the corner, and the clock on the wall ticked just loud enough to remind her that time was still moving, even when her chest felt frozen.

Aseeka sat curled on the leather couch, not in her usual upright, poised posture. Today, her body leaned toward the armrest, legs folded, a pillow clutched in her lap like armor. She hadn't said much for the first ten minutes of the session. She just sipped her tea. Stared at the rug.

Dr. Bruno didn't rush her. He never did.

"You're dodging," Dr. Bruno said flatly, scribbling something in his worn leather notebook.

Aseeka sat across from him, one leg crossed over the other, her arms folded tight like she was holding herself together with sheer willpower.

"I'm not dodging," she replied, voice clipped. "I'm tired."

Bruno looked up over the rim of his glasses, his expression unimpressed. "You're always tired when you don't wanna talk."

Aseeka rolled her eyes and sank deeper into the leather chair. "You ever think I might just be exhausted from carrying everybody's bullshit?"

Bruno didn't flinch. "You don't carry anyone's bullshit but your own. You consciously try to carry the world on your chest, but when will you realize you only have two hands?"

Silence stretched between them like a taut wire.

Finally, he spoke again, voice softer but razor-sharp. "You wanna know what I see when you walk in here, Aseeka?"

She didn't answer. Cause she didn't know if she was ready for his answer.

"I see a woman holding her breath. I see a little girl trying to outrun ghosts chasing her since she was old enough to understand what it meant to lose her father to the system. I see a judge so busy being strong for everyone else that she doesn't know how to sit still and bleed."

Her throat tightened, but she masked it with a smirk. "That's poetic."

"That's therapy," he shot back. "And I'm not the one who can't sleep at night."

He leaned forward, folding his hands. "You gonna tell me what's bothering you, or do I gotta keep pulling teeth?"

Aseeka hesitated, then let out a breath like she was deflating. "I got a case."

"You always got a case."

"This one's … personal."

Bruno's eyes sharpened. "How personal?"

She shook her head, her gaze falling to the carpet. "Someone I knew a long time ago. Someone who made me feel small."

Bruno sat back, letting that hang in the air. "And you're presiding?"

She nodded.

"That's dangerous."

"I know."

He studied her. "You gonna recuse yourself?"

Her jaw flexed. "I can't. Not yet. It's the Garvin case that the whole city is talking about, the gynecologist who harmed all those women during his so-called routine exams."

Bruno scribbled something down, then looked at her like he was looking straight through her.

"Listen to me, Aseeka. You've spent your whole damn life trying to control the narrative. But this? This case? It's not gonna let you. It's gonna crack you wide open if you're not careful."

Her throat worked around a lump she didn't want to acknowledge.

He leaned back, voice calm but deadly serious. "You don't deal with what's underneath all that power and polish; this case will deal with you."

She spoke slowly, feeling the tears welling in her eyes, "Dr. Bruno, I was one of those women." It was the first time she had said it out loud, and the tears began to fall down like rain.

"Is that why you requested this emergency meeting? Is this the thing that has been pressing on you since last week?" he said softly. "The Garvin case?"

She nodded slowly. Then swallowed hard. Her throat burned. She couldn't hold on to it anymore.

"I." She paused, blinking up at the ceiling like the words were stuck there. "I can't stop seeing the room."

Bruno waited, no pen scratching. No interruptions.

"The waiting room. That damn mural. The nurse. The magazines. The way everything looked so ... safe. It was like being wrapped in a lie. I didn't know I was inside." They sat in silence while Dr. Bruno listened to her sobs for a few minutes as he waited for her to say something.

She exhaled sharply, her voice brittle as she regained her composure. "I went to him for a check-up. Routine stuff. Breast exam. Pap smear. I was twenty-three. Law school was kicking my ass, and I figured ... this was one thing I could control. My health. My body."

She paused again. Something shifted in her eyes.

"But I wasn't in control."

Her hands gripped the pillow tightly.

"He touched me like I was his. Like I was something to explore, not examine. His fingers and his mouth moved slowly as if he were savoring it. Like he knew I wouldn't stop him. And I didn't. I felt so ashamed because, deep down, a piece of me felt like I enjoyed it. I even had an orgasm! Can you believe that shit?"

Dr. Bruno's jaw clenched just slightly. But he remained still. Anchored. Quiet.

"He told me I had 'perfect tissue elasticity.' Said my cervix looked beautiful. What the fuck kind of doctor says that?" Her voice cracked at the end, and for the first time in years, she let herself feel the weight of it. "But I didn't say anything. I pulled my clothes on and left as if nothing had happened. I told myself I was being dramatic. Sensitive. That maybe he didn't mean anything by it."

She covered her face with one hand. "But he did. I know he did."

Silence filled the room, thick and sacred.

Dr. Bruno leaned forward slightly, setting the notepad on the table beside him. "Thank you for trusting me with that, Aseeka. That wasn't your fault. Not a single part of it. And I want to confirm that sometimes people can be brought to orgasm when engaging in sexual misconduct; that does not make it consent. They are not synonymous."

She shook her head, tears continuing to slip free. "I'm a fucking Chief Judge. I put predators away every day. And I let him touch me like that."

"No," Bruno said, firm now. "You were a young woman in a vulnerable position, trusting someone who used that trust. That's not a weakness. That's survival. And now? You're reclaiming your power whenever you speak his name out loud."

She wiped her face roughly, her breath coming in shallow waves.

"I hate that I still remember how it felt," she whispered. "His voice. His fingers. The way he made me feel like I was overreacting while he was violating me. Telling me just to relax."

Dr. Bruno leaned back, eyes heavy with empathy and fire.

"Then let's give your memory something new, something truer. Let's build a space where your voice is louder than his shadow. We're not done with this, but we're starting."

And for the first time in over a decade, Aseeka Sinclair nodded, not because she believed she was healed.

But because she was ready to try.

Aseeka's voice came out low, almost broken. She wasn't crying anymore, but her eyes were still damp, like the storm had passed, but the ground was soaked.

She looked up at Dr. Bruno, her voice barely above a whisper.

"What will it feel like … when I heal from this shit?"

She said this shit like it was venom and glass and grief all at once, like the words themselves hurt to speak.

Dr. Bruno didn't answer right away. He let the silence stretch, not out of hesitation but reverence. Then, he leaned forward, elbows resting on his knees, and looked her dead in the eye. His voice was slow, deep, and deliberate, like reading scripture over drum beats.

"It'll feel like remembering who you were … before the world tried to convince you, you were broken.

Like breathing without permission.

Like peace that doesn't need proof to exist.

Like crying without shame, laughing without apology, and being touched without flinching.

It'll feel like your body finally belongs to you.

Like forgiveness, not for them, but for the parts of yourself you silenced to survive.

It'll feel like rage that doesn't destroy you but fuels you.

Like softness returning to your bones.

Like sleeping through the night.

Like looking in the mirror and not seeing a wound, but a woman who made it through a personal hell… and didn't leave her soul behind."

He let the words land.

Then added softer:

"Healing is when the memory stops holding the pen, and you get to write the rest of your story."

Aseeka sat still, her breath trembling.

She didn't have words.

But she didn't need them.

Because something cracked open inside her, and this time, it wasn't a break.

It was the beginning of a return.

Chapter 8: Malik, A Weight Carried in Silence.

The thing about always being the strong one, the funny one, the creative one, the fashionable one, the *fixer*, is that people forget you bleed, too.

Malik Stone leaned against the studio mirror, sweat dripping from his hairline, heart racing from the last eight-count. The room was still vibrating with the bass of Beyoncé's "Thique," but his body had already gone cold, not from exhaustion, but from *memory*.

He stared at his reflection: the beat-up Adidas, the Gucci belt, the designer durag, the Fenty highlight that caught the light just right. Flawless, as always. But behind his eyes? Tired. Fractured. Grieving.

He wiped his face and turned the music off, letting the silence wrap around him like a sheet. It was the only time he let himself fall apart. Alone. Between rehearsals. Between performances. Between brunches with the girls, he was expected to show up in full Malik Mode, sassy, sharp, and ready to roast a man to filth at a moment's notice.

But today... he couldn't shake the text from his mother: *Your uncle died. I didn't know how to tell you. I know y'all weren't close, but still ...*

He *had* been close. He's closer than he should've been. And that was the problem.

Malik had never told anyone what happened in that basement when he was nine, how his uncle used to whisper that it was *their little secret.* How the shame felt like acid in his chest every time someone said, "You were always such a sensitive little boy." How he learned to weaponize fashion and flair so no one would ever see the small, scared child behind the sequins.

Not even Aseeka knew. And she knew *everything.* And he knew everything about her. She was his go-to person. And he couldn't believe she finally told her therapist about Dr. Garvin. It inspired him to say his own truth out loud. He was having a hard time finding the courage, though.

They thought he was fearless. And maybe he was. But he was also walking around with unspoken grief tucked into the soles of his sneakers and rage pressed into the pleats of his Balenciaga.

Malik knew at a young age he liked boys, as did his parents and everyone else around him. He sat cross-legged on the wooden floor, wiping his palms on his thighs. His breath shook.

He remembered telling God he wouldn't let it define him. That he'd become *so fabulous,* so *flawless,* so *goddamn unforgettable,* that no one would ever pity him. And he did. He built an empire out of glitter and grit. Taught Black boys how to move their hips and hold their heads high. Choreographed liberation into eight-counts.

But tonight?

Tonight, he just wanted someone to *see him.* To not feel rendered invisible and have to cover it with a mask of strength and power.

To ask how he was. To stay when the room got heavy.

He thought of calling Aseeka to tell her the truth. But then he pictured her face, so much on her plate already. The case. Her father. Damon. All that silence.

So instead, he texted her a meme about Damon's bald spot and followed it up with, *"We still doing wine night Friday? I'll bring the petty."*

Because that's what Malik did, he showed up dressed to kill. Cracking jokes with wounds still open beneath his designer fit.

Because strength, for him, had never been about muscle or ego.

It was about surviving what no one saw and dancing through the pain.

But he desperately needed a friend, someone to see him without judgment or jokes to mask the hurt.

He sat down in the studio against the mirror. He felt as if, at times, it could see right through him. He always felt seen when he looked into it.

He looked at the sky and said, "Ancestors, I need you now. Put a rhythm in my heart and a move in my mind, letting me release this emotional burden. And if that's not the purpose, let me translate the pain into my art. I've heard it's the thing that will make me great one day. Can today be that day?"

He lowered his head and looked down at the gold-plated cross that was dangling from the 18-inch necklace on his chest, "Know there's something great coming, and if I should break along the way, Lordt, let the pieces of me that come back together be rooted in excellence and authenticity. Ashe."

And then his phone rang. Aseeka's name appeared on the screen, and he looked up to the sky, "OK, Lordt, answer me then!"

He answered the phone as enthusiastically as he could muster, "Hey, Gwerl, hey! What's up? I'm at the studio. Are you good?"

Aseeka answered, "I'm good. Do you want to meet me for a drink tonight? Like in the next hour at Limelight?"

Malik contemplated, "Yes, but I have a strange request. Can you and I just start, and then invite the girls after we've had a chance to converse? I need a space to talk, seriously. I think we both do, friend."

Aseeka could hear the pain in her friend's voice, "Yeah, love, I could use a similar space. We'll be each other's support system. Meet me at 10 p.m., and then we'll tell the girls to meet at 11:30 p.m. You know those bitches ain't goin' get there until 12:15-ish, sound good? I'll book us a private room."

He agreed, and they hung up.

And just like that, his ancestors answered, and he felt heard. Now, he needed to be seen, and Aseeka was the right friend to do that. The rest of the Gwerls were also great listeners, but Aseeka had a certain maturity and understanding. She knew how to listen without imposing her perspective or judgment, and that was precisely what he needed right now.

He grabbed his bag, headed home to get ready, and turned off the light in his studio, which had become his sanctuary. He turned and looked back in the room before walking out the door. He was grateful for his physical sanctuary and the comfort it brought. But he was starting to feel like something was missing in his life.

He thought that it was time to build up his mental sanctuary. A concept that was foreign to him as a survivor. But he thought if he could build a studio, surely he could build a steady mind.

One thing was for sure: he was ready to try. It was past due.

Chapter 9: Chanel, The Cost of Holding It All Together

The sound of Glavin's wail hit Chanel before she even stepped out of her Tesla. Galvin, her two-year-old daughter, was definitely a momma's girl and had a tendency to show out when she knew her mother was home. She had been sitting in it, just staring at her children, looking at her through the window for about 5 minutes while she played like she was on the phone. The front door was cracked, the porch light flickering like it had something to say, and the chaos inside was already building like a storm waiting to pop off. Chanel hated to admit that sometimes she hated coming home to a chaotic house, but she deeply loved her family. It felt wrong to even think it, but she would often just sit in the car and stare at the house, trying to muster up the energy to walk in and greet her family. A screaming child, a toddler who loved to play, a nagging nanny, and a difficult husband were not always her favorite things to face after a long day of dealing with indecisive clients. She had to remind herself that every day wasn't like this, but there were far more of them than she would have liked.

She walked into her house, a mid-century modern style home with 5,600 square feet of glass, soft neutrals, and intentional light, and immediately regretted it. Goldfish crackers were crushed into the rug she'd custom-woven in Morocco. Her three-year-old son, Jokeen, was in the middle of the open kitchen wearing nothing but a pull-up, holding a partly squashed banana like a microphone and screaming, "I pooped on the potty!" at the top of his lungs.

"Where's Gina?" Chanel muttered, kicking her heels off and tossing her bag on the counter.

"She left early. Said Glavin had a fever, but she cooled off," Markee's voice called from the living room. He was on the couch, feet up, with a PS5 controller in hand and *Call of Duty* lighting up the TV. "You ain't see my charger?"

"Markee." Her tone dropped. "You left two toddlers alone for thirty minutes?"

"First of all, it wasn't thirty," he snapped. "Second, I was right here. I could hear everything."

Glavin, her two-year-old daughter, wailed again from the upstairs hallway.

Chanel rushed past him without another word, scooped up her daughter, kissed her forehead, and whispered calming things until the baby settled against her shoulder. The fever was gone, but the tears weren't. She carried Glavin to her room, laid her down, and kissed her curls before returning downstairs.

She walked into the kitchen like a storm with no warning.

"I can't keep doing this, Markee," she said, voice low and deadly. "I can't."

He didn't look up. "Here we go."

"No. Here we go is me working 60 hours a week, running a multimillion-dollar design firm, keeping our kids alive, and coming home to your ass unemployed again."

"I had an interview last week," he muttered.

"You showed up late and didn't shave."

"I'm not gonna grovel for some finance, bro, at a job I don't want."

"No, you're just gonna sit on my couch, eat my groceries, and play video games like it's therapy."

Markee finally stood up, eyes flashing. "You think I wanna be this dude? Do you think this is who I planned to be? I was supposed to be somebody. I was on track to become a senior partner at one of the largest hedge funds in the Chi. But insulin costs money, and my mama was dying, and I made one bad choice trying to save her."

She paused. That landed. It always did.

But her voice didn't soften. "And she's gone, Markee. She's gone. And you've been punishing yourself, our children, and me ever since. If you were going to just sit on your ass and mope all day, you could have done that from a cell."

He looked stunned at what she said. She could see the hurt in his light brown eyes. He rubbed the back of his neck, pacing. "I can't believe you said that shit to me. I'm trying, Chanel. I swear to God I am. But you look at me like I'm another client project you can't fix. Like, I don't belong in your perfect little empire. I see you and your success; you remind me it's always yours. But you never talk about us building anything together. Instead, you spend more time tearing me down."

"I don't want to fix you," she said. "I want you to meet me. I want a partner. I want a man who can handle his own healing without leaving me to carry all the weight. I can't build with somebody who won't even attempt to go under his own construction, baby. It's like you won't even try."

Silence stretched.

Then, her phone buzzed.

Aseeka: Malik and I are hitting Limelight tonight. I got us a private room. Meet us there in 2 hours? Are you coming, or you gonna stay stuck in that house with your ghost of a man?"

"Yeah, let me get ready right quick. It should take me about 30 minutes to drive over there. She looked up at Markee as Gina, the nanny, walked back into the house. "Gina's back. I'm going out."

He scoffed. "Oh, so now you run the streets? Cool. Then I'm going out too. Travis is hitting a spot on the West Side."

"You mean the man who still wears throwbacks and sells fake Cartier on IG?"

Markee shrugged. "Whatever. If you're outside, I'm outside too."

She laughed. Cold. "Oh, you can stop playing Call of Duty to go out with your boys, but can't watch the kids. Enjoy that ego trip, Markee. Hope it fills the hole your purpose used to live in." She headed up the stairs to get ready.

He sighed, "I promise, I'm not going to take too much more of that kind of shit.

"Yeah, yeah," She yelled from the upstairs bathroom as she turned on the shower and started to undress to prepare for her outing with the Gwerls.

She didn't know what the night would bring. But she knew something was going to have to change real soon. She sometimes hated telling her friends about her life because they would judge her and not listen sometimes. It was fine when it was often her and Aseeka or Tasha talking. But the energy went from understanding to judgment when they all got together. She was eventually going to have to tell them how she was feeling. She was 41 years old, and it was way past time for her to speak up.

She would enjoy it tonight, but eventually must express how they made her feel. She decided to prepare for the night mentally.

When she hit the club, for the next few hours, she didn't have to be anyone's wife, anyone's savior, or anyone's reminder of what they lost.

She could just be.

Chapter 10: Saying It Out Loud

Aseeka had already uncorked the red when Malik buzzed up. They decided to meet at her house before heading to Limelight in case the emotions started to flow. Plus, the only private room she could get wasn't open for another two hours, so they had time, especially since it was walking distance from her house. He wore high-waisted leather pants, an oversized Balenciaga hoodie, and his signature gold hoops. But the energy behind his eyes was … off. Just slightly dimmed.

"You look like depression dipped in designer," she said, raising an eyebrow.

Malik smirked but didn't give her the usual read-back. He toed off his boots and flopped onto the couch like his bones weighed more than his body.

"You good?" she asked, grabbing two glasses, setting one on the coffee table, and sensing the heaviness on her friend's heart.

He shrugged. "I'm here; you good?" he said, sitting in her favorite couch chair, slouched down, staring through the glass patio doors with a beautiful Lake Michigan view. The door to the patio was slightly open, and you could hear the sounds of the water crashing against the rocks.

"That ain't what I asked."

Malik stared at the water for a beat. "Have you ever felt like you have been holding your breath for so long that you forgot what breathing feels like? Like you're drowning, even though you know how to swim?"

Aseeka didn't answer right away. She sat down beside him and pulled her knees up, resting her cheek on them.

"Every day."

They sat like that for a while. No TV. No music. Just the soft hum of the water outside her penthouse patio and the occasional creak of the leather chair when one of them shifted.

Finally, Malik said, "My uncle died. The one from back home."

She turned to him. "The preacher?"

He nodded.

"I'm sorry, Mal."

He paused. Then: "Don't be."

There was something about the way he said it. Quiet. Final.

She looked at him, looked at him, and saw the crack under the makeup. The child behind the confidence. The pain he hadn't named. And for once, she didn't fill the silence. She let him speak when he was ready.

"He hurt me," he said finally. "When I was little. I never told anybody."

Aseeka's stomach dropped. She knew this feeling all too well. Her hand instinctively reached for his, and he let her take it. The tears were starting to well up in her friend's eyes. She heard him swallow hard after he said it, watching his Adam's apple react to the swallow as his jaw tightened.

Malik laughed, but it was hollow. "And now he's dead. And I'm supposed to ... grieve? Celebrate? Forgive? I don't know what the fuck I'm supposed to feel."

"You feel whatever the hell you need to," she said. "You survived him. That's enough."

He looked at her, eyes glassy but steady. "You think it ever goes away? That shame?"

"No," she said honestly. "But it stops owning you. One day, you tell the truth enough times, and it starts sounding like freedom instead of failure."

They sat in silence again, fingers still interlocked.

"I'm proud of you for telling me," she said softly.

"I figured if *you* could finally tell Bruno what Garvin did," he said, voice cracking, "I could tell somebody too. You've always trusted me with your deepest secrets, and I love that about our friendship. If we didn't have a safe outlet, this would break us even more. "

Aseeka's eyes welled up, but she blinked fast. "We're not broken, Mal."

He nodded. "We just cracked open early."

Chapter 11: Tasha, The Things I Let Myself Feel

Tasha's back was arched, her 4C curls sticking to her neck as her breath slowed. Byron stood over her like Captain Morgan. Her head was hanging over the bed, and she was looking up at him while she sucked his dick. Tasha was a fellatio pro and enjoyed the position. She could even orgasm off the feeling of Byron's dick thrusting in and out of her mouth. Her saliva was running a bit down the side of her face due to the size of Byron's thick-ass, tight-skinned dick. He was moaning loudly, enjoying the moment while gently pinching her nipples every now and then. And on the other side of her, between her legs, dark skin glistening under the soft red lights of his penthouse bedroom, was Nini, gorgeous, legs like sculpture, skin like bronze silk, tracing lazy fingers along the curve of Tasha's thigh while she kissed her pussy lips. It was a full-on menage à trois. A part of their weekly routine. Byron was a freak, and he and Tasha would fuck almost every other day. And when they needed to spice things up, Nini was on speed dial. Like any other woman, they would pick up at his club, but Nini was a priority because she was the best.

Tasha grabbed the top of her head as she felt herself preparing to climax. But before she could come, Nini stood up, showing off the strap-on she had put on while devouring Tasha. She wrapped Tasha's legs around her thick chocolate thighs and slowly inserted the large strap-on into her wet-ass pussy. Tasha moaned out in pleasure at the unexpected penetration. But she couldn't say anything because she still had Byron's dick to deal with in her mouth. And now they were both moving in a rhythm that caused her body to thrust between the two of them. Nini had followed the pace of Byron moving his dick in and out of Tasha and replicated it in her pussy with the strap-on. Tasha was in ecstasy, feeling the shaft of Nini's strap-on and the shaft of Byron's dick simultaneously moving in and out of her body. Between the sounds of her pussy gushing and the sounds of her swallowing dick, she was about to lose control, and she knew it. And just as she was about to orgasm, Byron pulled his dick out of her mouth and squirted his hot cum all over her face. Before she could wipe her face off, she was in the midst of her own orgasm, thanks to Nini, who had her legs in the air as her knees gave out and her body twitched with pleasure.

"Damn, y'all trying to kill me," Byron mumbled, voice raspy with satisfaction. "This is how I wanna die." He handed Tasha a towel that he had sitting on the nightstand.

"Baby, this is how you live," Tasha purred, reaching for the silk robe at the foot of the bed.

Nini giggled, still high off the afterglow. "If this LA club hits like this night did, you better be prepared to file for spiritual insurance."

Tasha laughed, falling back onto the pillows, sweat-soaked and smiling. "You're an idiot."

But she was glowing.

This was her thing. Her joy. Her chaos. Her control. No labels. No guilt. Just *yes,* where she used to always say *no.*

Four years of this dance with Byron. A year after her divorce, she swore off monogamy and mediocrity in the same breath. Byron came with both hands full: sex, power, ambition, and a club empire that never slept. They weren't in love, not in the traditional sense. But they were aligned. And when he introduced Nini last year, things got even more ... interesting.

Byron turned his head, grinning. "So ... y'all gonna come out to LA for the opening or nah? I'm talking private jet, rooftop suite, and a velvet-rope-type of night. VIP treatment for my two queens."

"You mean me and Nini?" Tasha teased.

He smirked. "I mean ... you and Aseeka."

Tasha's face shifted. Barely. But Nini caught it.

"Mmhmm," Nini hummed, rolling to the edge of the bed. "Here comes the drama."

"It's not drama," Tasha said, reaching for her water. "It's awareness. He's got a little crush, that's all."

Byron held his hands up. "She's beautiful. Powerful. Smart. I'm human. You know she's fine as hell, and I gotta hit that just once."

"You're predictable," Tasha said, sipping. "You always want a goddess and a gladiator."

Before Byron could answer, Tasha's phone buzzed on the nightstand. She reached for it and saw Aseeka's name flash across the screen.

She grinned.

"Speak of the power suit," she muttered and answered on speaker. "Go 'head, Supreme."

Aseeka's voice crackled through. "What are you doing?"

"Recovering."

"Ugh, you're nasty. We're hitting the club tonight: Malik, Chanel, and I. Ima call Bri next. You rolling or nah?"

Byron and Nini both perked up like teenagers eavesdropping on gossip.

Tasha grinned. "I mean, I *was* gonna stay in and let my spirit realign after that holy trinity of a session ... but y'all know I can't miss a good mess."

"Good," Aseeka said. "We are leaving in an hour. And tell your sex cult I said hey."

Tasha spoke like an enthusiastic teenager, "Ok, bish, plus I have an update about Crave, it just made it to the final round of FDA approval. Shit is bout to be lit!"

Click.

Tasha fell back into the pillows, cackling.

"You heard her," she said. "Wrap this up. Mama's got eyeliner to smudge and a reputation to protect."

Byron leaned shirtless against the bathroom door wall, sipping a green drink slow like whiskey and watching Tasha scroll through the latest batch of Crave test results on her tablet. "You realize if this shit gets FDA-approved, you're about to be the Black Dr. Ruth meets Rihanna, right?" he smirked.

Tasha didn't look up; she just tapped her screen and smiled. "Correction: I'm already that. Approval just makes it legal."

He chuckled, stepping closer. "You built a pill that turns people into waterfalls and walking hard-ons. That's iconic."

She finally looked up, eyes sharp with mischief. "I built a pill that helps people stop pretending they're not hungry for more. Desire shouldn't be taboo. It should be intentional." Byron raised a brow, impressed, and turned on all over again. "Remind me why I'm not asking for a lifetime supply?"

"Because you already stay turned on," she said, leaning in, "but when Crave drops? The world won't be ready for what we unlock. I can't wait to introduce it at the opening in LA."

Nini was already grabbing her things. "One day, I want to be like y'all when I grow up; see y'all later; I gotta be at the strip club in 45 minutes. The heavy hitters will be in VIP tonight after the all-star weekend; that's a 20K night for your girl," she stated before exiting.

Byron pulled the sheet over his head. "I'm gonna miss you tonight."

Tasha leaned over and kissed his forehead. "Then behave. Or don't. But either way, I'll be back when I'm good and ready."

She slid off the bed, hips swaying, confidence dripping off her like sweat.

Tasha wasn't running from anything anymore.

She was running *toward* it.

Chapter 12: Brielle, A Love That Works Because We Did

The leather interior of the Range Rover smelled like a new car and new money. Brielle had one heel off, her bare foot resting on the dash, a silk wrap protecting her curls, and a glassy smirk on her face as Kenneth merged onto Lake Shore Drive with the smoothness of a man who never rushed for anything but her.

"That pitch was flawless, baby," she said, sipping the last sparkling water. "You had old boy sweating through his designer linen."

Kenneth chuckled; he looked good in his crisp pink polo, CMB Denim & Heritage Goods jeans, and freshly twisted locs. Kenneth was a real one from the Bronx who grew up a hustler but redirected his hustling skills to become a high-powered businessman. She fell in love looking at him, always rooted in authenticity but knowing how to build his table. His fucking swagger was constantly on 100, one hand on the wheel, the other resting casually on her thigh. "Because he didn't expect me to come with projections and personality. They're used to numbers. Not vision."

"And a fine-ass Black man serving it on a silver tray," she added, glancing over at him. "You showed out tonight."

He turned toward her briefly, that slow-burning smile that still melted her after all these years. "I always show out when my girl's in the room," he said, sliding his hand up her thigh and gently rubbing the slit between her pussy lips.

He realized she wasn't wearing any panties, and that turned him on even more.

She grinned and rolled her eyes, feeling turned on by her husband's forwardness as she felt the gentle touch from his index finger rubbing on her clit, "You're lucky I already married you."

"Twice, technically. Should I pull over?"

She laughed. "Vegas does not count. And yeah." They were right by his office. "Pull into the garage at your office; I am feeling spontaneous," she said as she reached over and started rubbing the emerging bulge in his pants.

They cruised silently for a beat until they reached the garage. He pulled out his card to buzz the car in, and the gate opened. It was late at night, so no one was at work except the security guard who managed the building. Kenneth pulled the Range Rover into his private parking spot. He felt the adrenaline rushing through his body as his wife's French-manicured hand began pulling his dick out of his jeans. He was fully erect and ready.

"I'm about to fuck the shit out of you," he muttered. He and Bri loved to have sex in random-ass places. Though they had been married for 10 years, the passion had never left.

"No, you're not; Ima suck the life out of that dick. You just landed that amazing deal, and you look good AF; tonight is about you," Bri murmured.

She grabbed a piece of ice from her cup of soda water and positioned herself over the console in the middle of the Range Rover that separated their seats. As she hiked up her dress, exposing her ass, she knew that her husband knew what to do while she pleased him. Her titties fell out of her dress and pressed against his leg. No instructions are needed.

She slowly took the head of his dick and gently sucked it in her mouth, letting the ice slide around the tip. The sound of Kenneth's moans made her excited. She began slowly moving his dick deeper in and out of her mouth. She could smell his Calvin Klein cologne as she felt his hard-ass dick moving in and out of her mouth. Then slowly, she felt his hand running down the crack of her ass to her pussy lips. He pushed his two fingers inside of her and started to slowly move them in and out of her while she continued to suck his dick.

She could taste his precum shooting out, exciting her. She started to speed up just enough for him to begin losing control. Kenneth had his head laid back, his fingers gently darting in and out of her pussy that was growing wetter and wetter by the minute. He was moaning loudly now as he could hear subtle moans from his wife. The ice was taking him to a new level of pleasure. He begged her to stop because he wanted to put her in the back seat and fuck her brains out, but the feeling of her warm mouth mixed with the cold ice was sending him. Before he could stop, he felt himself about to explode. It was like Bri knew, and she started sucking harder, causing him to moan out loudly as his back was arched entirely.

Bri enjoyed swallowing her husband's cum. He was a carnivore, so it tasted bitter, but she didn't care. He often gave spectacular head; she had to teach him, but tonight was his night. And she could have an orgasm just sucking his dick, and she did. His fingers darting gently and forcefully in and out of her pussy helped the moment along, but still. She loved him and loved how much they loved pleasing each other. There was nothing to clean up since Bri swallowed it all. She leaned back into her seat, pulled down the mirror from overhead, fixed the curls on her lace front, and then fixed her makeup. Meanwhile, Kenneth was sitting in the driver's seat, regaining his composure.

She chuckled, "You OK over there, sport? You need some help, boo?"

Kenneth took a deep breath and stared at her smirkingly, "Naw, son, I'm good; give me a minute, though."

He then started up the car again and pulled out of the driveway, waving to the security guard and walking around outside the building, conducting his rounds.

The city lights were painting the windshield in gold and purple hues. Bri reflected on how far she and Kenneth had come in their marriage, and the long nights of the debate over whether or not to have children hadn't always been easy. It was easy with him now, *earned* ease. Years of therapy, late-night fights, hard truths, and soft touches. They'd done the work. They had the scars to prove it.

Then her phone buzzed.

Aseeka: *Don't be a grandma tonight. We're hitting the club. Malik said to wear heels. You can throw at a man if needed.*

Brielle smirked and showed the screen to Kenneth.

"Trouble?"

"Only the best kind. The Gwerls are out at Limelight tonight. You good to drop me?"

He glanced at the GPS and then adjusted the location. "You're five minutes away. Of course."

She leaned over and kissed his cheek. "I love you."

"More than those ridiculous boots you wore last weekend?"

"Let's not be dramatic."

He chuckled again and reached for her hand, kissing it slowly. "Have fun. But remember, if you end up bailing anyone out, it's your name on the paperwork this time."

"No promises."

Chapter 13: Syd and The Verses Unveiled

Syd sat cross-legged on the floor of their modest apartment, surrounded by a sea of crumpled lyric sheets and half-empty coffee cups. They had just popped an edible, and they were waiting for it to kick in; it had been a long day, and the Hennessey Syd enjoyed wasn't enough to help release the lingering discomfort that sat on their heart. The soft glow of a single lamp cast elongated shadows, mirroring the complexities of their thoughts. In honor of Transgender Day of Visibility, Syd was crafting a song titled "Hiding," a poignant reflection of their journey.

As they strummed their guitar, a line emerged:

"In the mirror's reflection, a truth untold …"

The words struck a chord deep within, prompting Syd to pause. Their life was a tapestry woven with threads of resilience and secrecy. By day, Syd was a passionate songwriter, pouring their soul into melodies that spoke of love, identity, and freedom. Syd was highly successful at their job as a ghostwriter and made good money. But also struggled with the challenge of many homophobic ass artists not wanting to work with them in public but loving their musical talent. Fuck them, they thought, they could write for people who don't give a fuck, and be perfectly happy. The only challenge is that they would make a lot less money. To supplement income, they navigated the clandestine world of sex work, a reality they concealed from even their closest friends.

It was continuously disappointing to try to find a safe space to work due to the stigma of ignorance that trans populations faced. Syd completed their undergraduate work in music, with a minor in economics, specifically focusing on trans stats. The statistics were stark and unrelenting. The facts played over and over in their head daily. They thought about the studies that revealed that transgender individuals, particularly Black trans women, faced disproportionate challenges. The most pressing one was economic hardships. Approximately 13 percent of transgender Americans have engaged in sex work, with figures rising to 44 percent among Black transgender individuals.

They felt their inner anger rise as they thought about all the trans friends whose lives were taken too soon due to hate and bigotry. Transphobia was no fucking joke, especially among the Black community. Their mind quickly flashed to the stats of violence and mortality for trans populations. They had read that between 2017 and 2023, there were 263 homicides of transgender or gender-expansive individuals in the U.S., with Black trans women comprising a significant portion of these victims.

Syd was acutely aware of these realities. Their involvement in sex work was facilitated through a private site that prioritized discretion, allowing them to earn a living while minimizing exposure. Yet, this path was fraught with complexities.

Recently, Syd had been involved with a potential partner, Shawn, whom they'd met at a coffee shop, a man whose touch ignited a blend of desire and trepidation.

That day, he wore a light blue button-up with dark blue slacks, and his cognac shoes matched his cognac shirt. He wore a gold Rolex Submariner on his right wrist. His curly black hair was freshly tapered, not to mention his beautiful ass smile, and his thick ass pink lips didn't hurt the visual situation either. When they met eyes, he slowly approached Sydney, who had finished ordering her drip Americano coffee and was now waiting for it at the side counter behind a long list of other orders. He had corporate written all over him as he kept checking his watch. It was clear he was waiting there for a meeting. Syd had never felt this kind of immediate attraction to anyone.

It felt like love at first sight, and it all happened so fast they didn't have time to tell Shawn's fine ass anything. They recalled seeing Shawn's hazel eyes staring at them from across the room while they were ordering at the counter. But then again, why the fuck should she have to, they thought. Shawn hadn't said whether he was into trans women or not until their phone call the next day. Fuck, they thought, they should tell him right then and there, but the attraction was so strong. Their encounters had been limited to intimate acts, with Syd carefully sidestepping full disclosure of their transgender identity. The man's escalating requests for deeper intimacy weighed heavily on Syd's conscience. The fear of rejection, or worse, violence, loomed large. Syd often struggled with the safety line between revealing their identity and missing out on what could be love if people weren't so ignorant and trapped in the confines of heteronormativity. Syd grew frustrated and decided to move to their bedroom; it was where they did some of their best work, both creatively and sexually.

Syd turned on an instrumental they received from their favorite engineer, Blocko, an up-and-coming producer from the South Side. The beat looped softly through the speakers, slow and aching like the ache behind their ribs. Syd sat at the edge of their bed, laptop open, fingers hovering over the keyboard, but the lyrics wouldn't come. Not yet.

They'd been working on this song for weeks. "*Hiding.*" Written for Trans Day of Awareness. For the girls who didn't make it. For the ones still breathing but barely living. For themself.

They sat on the edge of the bed and closed their eyes, hoping for a creative word to come through them. The clandestine meetings, the stolen moments of connection, and the ever-present shadow of unspoken truths. The lyrics of "Hiding" began to take shape, echoing their internal conflict. They ran a hand over their scalp and stared at the blinking cursor. The hook was there beneath the surface:

I show you pieces you can't name,
But you still don't see me.
You kiss the lips, not the truth,
And I'm still hiding ... in plain sight.

The last line made their chest tighten.

Because it wasn't just a song; it was a truth that societal norms forced into a confession.

Syd had been seeing Shawn for the past two weeks and was feeling him. Casual. Discreet. A fine-ass man with a mouth that lay just right and hands that knew where to go. They'd only fooled around. Oral, mostly. Safe, familiar territory. The kind of half-truths that kept things soft. But he didn't know. He didn't know *they* were trans. He didn't know how dangerous his curiosity could turn if the truth ever rose to the surface.

He'd been pressuring them for sex lately. Not in a violent way. But insistent. Repetitive. *"You trust me or not?"* he asked two nights ago, kissing them like love and ignorance were the same thing.

Syd didn't trust easily, especially not with their body.

Especially not in this world.

Their statistically captivated brain recited the numbers again: *Black trans women are murdered at staggeringly high rates*, many of them by men they once trusted. In 2022 alone, at least 38 trans people were murdered in the U.S., the majority Black women, and those are only the names we *know*. Discretion wasn't just a business practice. It was survival.

They shifted on the mattress, glancing at the little velvet box on the dresser where they kept their cash. Sex work wasn't their whole life, but it funded freedom. It paid for studio time, soft sheets, and nights that didn't end in fear.

Through a private site with NDAs and no bullshit, Syd found a way to own their body while keeping the world at a distance.

But secrets stack.

And tonight, they felt heavy. At that moment, the first line came to Syd like a ton of bricks.

Masked by moonlight, secrets we keep ...

The sudden vibration of their phone jolted Syd from their reverie. Aseeka's name flashed on the screen. Syd answered, annoyed that Aseeka was disturbing her creative juices as they were just beginning to flow, "What bitch?"

"Get your ass to the club. We need you here."

Syd smirked and rolled their eyes.

"Bitch, don't make me come drag you outta that emotional songwriter hole. Limelight. Tonight. Everybody's going. Put on something that says, 'Yes, I write pain, but I'm still THAT Gwerl.'"

They stared at the screen for a beat, then exhaled and smiled.

Sometimes, being seen didn't start with the truth.

Sometimes, it started with glitter.

"Tonight," they whispered to themselves, "we dance. Tomorrow, we face the music."

Chapter 14: Limelight: Fuck It Friday Energy

The line outside Limelight wrapped around the block like Black prom night in July. The bass thumped hard enough to make the sidewalk vibrate, even before you got to the velvet ropes. Neon-purple lighting illuminated the entrance, and Limelight's gold script sign glowed like a crown above the double doors.

Inside was organized chaos: dancers grinding under flickering lights, bodies moving like sin and salvation were the same damn thing. The DJ booth pulsed at the front of the dancefloor, blasting a remix of old-school Busta Rhymes and Megan Thee Stallion while servers in crop tops and combat boots weaved between clusters of beautiful Black people sipping from glowing glasses.

Aseeka and Malik walked in first, flashing VIP wristbands and skipping the chaos of coat check, already dressed like they owned the building. Malik served *casual flamboyance,* rocking sheer black with gold accents, rings on every finger, and a fan tucked in his back pocket. Aseeka strutted in beside him in a chocolate brown jumpsuit that hugged her curves like velvet prayer, her heels clicking like warning shots.

"Where's the Drift Room?" Malik asked, lips glossy, eyes scanning the staircase that spiraled upward like a champagne flute turned upside down.

A sharply dressed host appeared like magic. "Right this way. Ms. Sinclair, welcome back."

The Drift Room sat on the second floor, part of a circular
layout of private suites that hovered over the dancefloor
like gods peeking down from Olympus. Each room had
windows that could be slid open to let the music and energy
pour in or closed for low-key privacy. Soundproof. Sexy.
Sophisticated.

The Drift Room was a vibe: deep leather couches in
caramel and onyx, velvet accent chairs, low golden
lighting, and glass panels offering a full view of the chaos
below. A chrome and glass mini-bar sat on one end, already
stocked with mixers, lime wedges, and ice. On the marble
table: Veuve Clicquot, White Hennessy, and El Pintor
tequila, each bottle chilled and ready for bad decisions.

Malik walked in first and flopped dramatically onto the
nearest chair. "Oh, this is grown and *trifling*. I love it."

Aseeka smirked and cracked the window just an inch—
enough for the beat to sneak in and wrap around them like a
hug.

One by one, the rest of the Gwerls trickled in.

Chanel arrived next, her heels clicking like punctuation, her
face beating and her aura exuding, "Don't ask me about my
husband." She wore gold hoops and a jumpsuit so sharp it
could file taxes. She was escorted up by a server carrying
her lemon drop with a Tajín rim, just how she liked it.

Tasha came in laughing, talking shit on the phone, wearing
a silver mesh dress with a thigh slit and zero apologies. She

air-kissed everyone and headed straight for the Veuve, pouring her glass like she paid rent here.

Syd was the last to walk in, quiet, smooth, and layered in all black with a bold red lip and a look in their eye that said *I'm here, but I'm carrying something.* No one asked. They hugged. Kissed cheeks. Passed them the Henny. Let them exist in the room without having to perform.

The room felt like a ritual. The clink of glasses. The deep laugh from the belly. The DJ screamed, *"Y'ALL READY TO ACT STUPID OR WHAT?!"*

And the Gwerls, every last one of them, raised their glasses like prayer and shouted, "Yasssssss!"

"To Fuck It Fridays," Malik said, standing up with his glass.
 "To being fine, free, and completely fed the fuck up."

They cheered. Loud. Without fear.

Chanel's stomach growled, "I'm hungry. What's up with some appetizers or something?"

Malik took the iPad off the wall and handed it to her. Get me those sweet potato cornbread muffins and some seared pork belly.

Chanel rolled her eyes. "First of all, the iPad is in your hand. Order it yourself, and secondly, order mine too!

Malik turned swiftly and looked Chanel up and down, "Ooop! For that, Ima order your ass a bowl of olives and a salad."

Chanel hated olives, one of her least favorite foods in the world, and everybody knew it. "Get faaacked up playing with me," she said as she threw back her drink. "Them sweet potato muffins be hittin, and add some bang bang shrimp, sir!"

Malik started ordering, "Ok, fine, but I'm going to eat half of your shit when it gets here; anybody else want anything?"

Chanel looked at him with a serious face, "I want my fucking marriage to work and not feel like it's falling apart," she dropped her head and felt the tears starting to form.

The whole group was now quiet and focused on Chanel. Tasha put her hand on her shoulder, "We listen, and we don't judge what the fuck is going on."

Syd sat straight up, "Wait a second, I know he bet not have put his hands on you, cause bitch I will take off these heels and lace up the Jordans and go to work! Just say the word." Syd put her glass down and leaned forward. "Want me to kill him? What's the life insurance rate giving?"

"Shut up, fool," Aseeka said as she handed Chanel another drink. "You heard Tasha, we listen, and we don't judge, tell us what's up. I know we be giving you a hard time sometimes, but in all seriousness, jokes aside, we're here.

Malik sat down next to her and immediately "I mean, gotdamn y'all, why can't Markee just get his shit together and get off his fucking ass," he was trying to help the situation.

Bri gave him a rugged look, "Malik! Let her speak."

Chanel raised her head and looked around. "No, he's right. Markee says he's been looking for a job but can't find anything. And when I come home from work, he's always playing the game and barely engaging with the kids. It's like we don't even exist to him sometimes. We don't have sex the way we used to, and he says it's cause he's depressed. I know he would never cheat on me, but gotdamn. That shit got me feeling insecure AF."

Aseeka said, "Yeah, you've been saying for a while, he's been like that. You know I don't care much for his ass, and I'm not trying to justify his actions, but do you think he's depressed? You know prison does such a number on our mental health, and I advise people to go and get counseling after they are released and while they're locked up."

Chanel started to cry even harder, "He hasn't been the same since he went in there, y'all. It changed him. Like it took the life out of him, you know, his hopes, his dreams, they all feel gone."

Tasha put her hand under Chanel's chin and lifted her head up, "You know I don't care much for Markee, but I know how much you love him. I also know how much you want your marriage to work. Byron has a Black male support group that might be beneficial for him. I can put in a good word."

Chanel nodded, "Yeah, I think he might like that. It could get him around some strong Black men doing something with their lives."

Aseeka looked up as if she suddenly realized, "Oh yeah, Byron is a part of that; he loves it!"

Syd paused, "Wait, a bunch of fine ass, successful Black men sitting around supporting one another, this ain't a code for a Circ Jerk, is it? If so, send me an invite; I'm into it."

Malik enthusiastically agreed, "Ok, bitch, I'm in!"

Tasha laughed, "As freaky as Byron's ass is, he doesn't like dick, so I doubt it. But why don't the two of y'all start your own little jerk-off session and invite me so I can watch? You know I like watching that shit."

Malik, "I almost slapped the lace front off you just now; you know I like masculine brothers; Syd can keep them titties too themselves!"

Syd jumped up and motorboated Malik.

Malik came up smiling, "Ok, never mind, I might be into it cause the titties are nice!"

The whole group laughed loudly.

Tasha focused back on Chanel, "I will text Byron in the morning and tell him to send me the information for the group. And I'll let you send it to you ASAP. I believe they meet on Monday nights. If Markee needs some convincing, I can have Byron reach out directly."

Aseeka joined in, "Actually, Markee and Damon hoop together at the gym on Saturdays. I can tell Damon to invite him, and I bet that would be better since they know each other."

Chanel was overwhelmed with gratitude, "Ok, I would appreciate that. I love y'all so much. Thank you for being my friends."

Tasha said softly, "We're not friends; we're family, baby, and that's what family does."

Syd reached for their phone as it went off. It was a text from Shawn.

Shawn: I know you are out with your Gwerls, but hit me up after the club. I really want to see you tonight, babe.

Syd sat back and took a big gulp of their whisky, checking their thoughts about their relationship with Shawn; it weighed on her. They needed to talk about it, "Can we continue to listen, and not judge? I got some shit I need to talk about."

Bri, "Where did you hide the body? Let me call Kenneth and the homies!"

Syd chuckled, "It's not like that, but Ima keep that in mind if and when I do kill a muthafucka over one of you bitches! Keep that option open for me, boo!"

Bri laughed and sipped her drink, "And done now, what's up?"

Syd stared into space, " I met this dude who approached me at the coffee shop, and when I tell you, he is the finest thing I've ever seen. It was like love at first sight. We have been talking for about a month now. And we're hitting it off—the connection is strong as fuck."

Before they could finish, Malik chimed in, "But does he know that you're trans?"

Syd immediately felt a wave of sadness, fear, and shame, "No, but I have been sucking his dick on the regular.

Aseeka felt a wave of fear come over her for Syd, "Sydney …no the fuck you didn't! You know how dangerous that shit is! I just dealt with a case where a dude killed a trans woman for something similar!"

Syd was now defensive, "I know, OK! I fucking know, but why does it have to be like that, y'all? Why can't we just have a healthy-ass relationship? Why can't I love who I want to love?

Because that's not our society, and some people aren't willing to accept it," Bri chimed in on the conversation.

Tasha started to feel a bit annoyed, "That's not what this shit right here is about. I fully support trans women as women, but there are some limitations. You should've told him up front, sent him a fucking text or something. You are misleading him. That's wrong."

Syd felt themselves growing angry with Tasha's statement, "How the fuck can you love me with limits, and I don't expect y'all to get it fully? Ya'll were born with the privilege of being in the right body and being able to be your authentic self. My shit different."

Chanel decided to be the voice of reason, "We are not judging you, baby; I think we are more fearful of you. In most situations like this, you don't know if you're safe even if you tell him up front. Yeah, he might be attracted to you mentally and physically, but you don't know that if he doesn't know you fully physically. "

Malik was mad at Syd for putting themselves in the situation in the first place, "Because the truth is you need to tell the man, and have you asked him if he is heterosexual? Maybe he likes trans women, you never know in this fucking world."

Syd felt their hearts sync again, "Yeah, he is 35, and he wants a wife and kids. He has talked about the women he's dated in the past."

Malik's eyes widened, "Oooh shit, this is a messy one, bitch. You gotta tell him. The good thing is you've got hands; just make sure you are in a public place or even text it to him. Hell, do we know if he's mentally unstable?"

Aseeka sat up, "I know, right? Give me his name and birthdate, and I will look his ass up ASAP!"

Syd laughed, "I know y'all trying to be there for me, but damn this ain't helping. It felt good to get it off my chest, but now I am even more worried. I will figure it out and keep y'all posted."

Malik said supportively, "If you need anything, let me know. I will be there when you tell him. I could hide off in the distance behind a newspaper, but be close enough to pounce on a nigga if you necessary, gotdamnit!"

Malik pounced on Bri, and they all laughed as Bri tried to push him off.

The speakers erupted with Juvenile's "Back That Azz Up!"

Malik started popping his booty on Bri.

Bri put her hand on Malik's butt. "Get off me before I stick my finger in that little muscular thang!"

Malik became intrigued, "Don't threaten me with a good time bitch!"

Aseeka jumped up and started moving her body to the music, "Y'all wanna head downstairs and dance?"

"Yaaaasssss," they all chimed in, making their way to the exit door and heading down to the dance floor.

Tasha grabbed the iPad and ordered another round of drinks so it would be waiting for them when they returned to the room.

The six of them danced together in a circle. Malik often hopped in the middle while the rest cheered on his antics. As a dancer, Malik knew precisely how to show out on the dance floor. All of them had a good rhythm and enjoyed the moment. The dance floor was pretty packed but not overwhelming. The sounds of '90s and 2000s hip-hop helped to make the vibe lit. The club had great lighting and two floors. It was about 10,000 square feet, not including the amenities attached to it, like the restaurant. But it had three rooms you could patronize: the room that played house music, the themed room of the night, and a karaoke section. Limelight had spotlights going all around the club, and if one landed on you, it was your moment to show the fuck out. You were literally in the limelight. You would appear on the six 85-inch screens around the club, mounted to the ceiling. As they danced, the Limelight shined on Malik, and immediately he did what he always does and showed the fuck out. The whole club was cheering as Malik did his thang and started clapping to "Ante Up," which was now blaring over the speakers.

Once Malik finished his dance, they returned to their reserved room. As they made their way to the staircase, Malik saw a familiar face. A guy he had once ghosted, Skylar, was waving him down. Malik recognized Skylar and immediately shot up the stairs like a bat out of hell. The Gwerls were surprised and had no idea what was happening, but followed after Malik in a hurry. Malik took two to three steps at a time until he reached the room, where he rushed them all in. He then stood against the door with a look of extreme horror as he faced the girls.

Aseeka stayed calm because she knew Malik tended to overreact, "What the fuck just happened?"

Tasha stared at Malik, "You saw one of your gotdamn jump-offs again, didn't you?"

Malik looked horrified, "Ssshhhhh the fuck up! Do y'all think he saw us?"

Sydney had gone in their bag and pulled out some brass knuckles; placing them on and taking off their heels, they stated, "Who do we have to fuck up?"

Bri looked at Malik, "First of all, who the fuck is *he,*" and I'm sure he did. Besides you shaking your ass on the big screen, it was obvious to see your long-legged ass running upstairs like it was an Olympic sport!"

Chanel stared at Malik, "The person waving at you? Oh yeah, bitch, I'm sure he saw you. Now the fuck is him?"

Malik slid down to the floor. "He is Skylar, and I met him on a gay dating app. It started off cool, we got along great, and then.." Malik's head dropped as if he were hiding a deep shame.

Tasha yelled out in anticipation, "Then what bitch, spit it out."

Malik spoke with extreme disappointment, "Then we finally met up, and I was about to let him get all in this thang. And this muthafucka dick fished me y'all. He had a micro penis! I couldn't believe my damn eyes. And y'all know I will top or bottom; I'm an equal opportunist. But I was so turned off, I left immediately and never said a word to him again. Blocked his ass and everything."

A slight pause came over the room, and then everyone laughed.

Sydney put their heels back on and their brass knuckles back in their purse. They grabbed the El Pintor tequila bottle and started fixing themselves a drink.

Malik still looked afraid. "We can't leave until he's gone."

Aseeka laughed, "Bitch, we gon' leave when we're ready to leave. Just tell him you lost interest if he approaches you."

Syd spoke with a playful but serious tone, "And if he can't understand that, he will be handled accordingly."

Chanel said snarkily, "Cause that wasn't clear when you took one look at his dick and high knees and butt kicks pursued."

Malik ran to the balcony to see if Skylar had followed them. But to his comfort, there was no sign of Skylar anywhere. He felt himself calming down and decided to rejoin the girls and make a drink. The food had also arrived and was waiting for them beside the alcohol on the table.

They all relaxed, indulged in the numerous appetizers and drinks, and vibed to the music as the night unfolded.

Aseeka asked the group, "What y'all got planned this weekend?"

Bri answered, "The kids have games, so we've got flag football and T-ball tournaments all weekend."

Tasha answered next, "I'm still helping Byron with the LA opening, so I'll be helping with the plans at his spot."

Chanel chimed in, "I'm working tomorrow. I'm helping to create the upgrades for the new hockey stadium, and then I'll have Sunday dinner with the family. Markee's parents are hosting it."

Aseeka suddenly remembered, "Oh yeah, I have dinner with the family this Sunday, too. My mom said she has a surprise for us. Tomorrow, I don't plan on doing shit. My ass goin' be hiding and recovering from tonight and this long as week."

"Same," Syd stated as they threw back their drink. "I gotta figure out how to break the news to Shawn." Syd could feel the fear sitting in their chest as they said it out loud.

Malik looked at Syd, "We're here if you need us. Cause my ass will be hiding as well from all the micro penises in the world!" He said as he inhaled his glass of champagne.

Bri shook her head and chuckled. She considered how much she appreciated marriage and how hard dating was, especially in your 40s. Even to have a happy marriage these days was a blessing. She looked around at all of her friends in admiration. They still loved each other after all these years.

Aseeka was also looking around at all of her friends. She realized how much she appreciated them and their willingness to be a safe space for one another. And she loved that they always made time for one another. She walked over to the balcony and looked down at the rest of the club as she sipped her drink. She heard the DJ announce the last call.

She reflected on the authenticity and love in their group. Were they perfect? No, not by any means, but they were her soulmates. Each one brings a different and necessary life experience to the table.

She thought to herself, up here, overlooking the world they'd spent their whole lives surviving, they weren't hiding.

They were exactly who they said they were, for the most part.

Chapter 15: Soul to Sole, The Family Dinner

The smell of fried chicken, collard greens, and fresh cornbread filled Monica Sinclair's tiny South Side kitchen like a warm hug Aseeka wasn't ready for.

She stood outside the front door for a full minute before pulling out her key to let herself in, adjusting her energy like armor.

Family dinners were always a gamble, laughter, love, and at least three side arguments guaranteed.

When the door swung open, her older sister Shanice was already talking.

"Bout damn time, Little Miss Federal Judge," Shanice teased, pulling her in for a hug that smelled like hair oil and Chanel No. 5.

"Sup, baby sis," Marcus said from the couch, barely looking up from the game on TV.

The oldest, Anthony, was already stirring something on the stove, playing his usual role as Mama's right hand.

The Sinclair house smelled like collard greens, roasted garlic, and secrets waiting to be told.

The dining room buzzed with that familiar sibling rhythm, teasing, side-eyes, and one-upmanship wrapped in love and a minor trauma. Their mother had set the table like it was Sunday dinner in the '90s: mismatched wine glasses, folded cloth napkins, a lemon pound cake half-covered in foil at the center like a holy relic. Their mother's pound cake could bring instant happiness to anyone's face. The sour taste of lemon, mixed with just the right sweetness and moisture, instantly melted in your mouth. Just thinking about it made her family's mouth water.

Aseeka sat near the head of the table, legs crossed, dressed in a tailored burnt orange two-piece, her edges laid, and her nails speaking quiet luxury. She sipped on a glass of red, watching her brothers bicker like it was 1998.

Anthony, the oldest at 49, leaned back in the chair he always claimed as his. He was built like the former athlete they all knew him to be, still broad-shouldered, still walking like a man who'd broken a few ankles on the court. He now ran a youth mentorship program and had traded trash talk for TED Talks, but the little brother energy still lived in his grin.

"Man, my kids only call me when they need shoes or somebody to cosign something," he said, chuckling. "I swear they think I'm running Foot Locker and Experian out my back pocket." He was a great father, but unfortunately, he and the mother of his two children had irreconcilable differences. Aseeka reflected on how she told him not to marry that dumb bitch, but he wouldn't listen. He was blinded by love and felt obligated because he got her pregnant. The family felt she was only watching him go to the league. And when his college career ended after he tore both ACLs, she showed her true colors. Aseeka felt slightly sad reflecting on how her brother dealt with the transition. He went to a dark place for a while but found his way out of it through therapy and his family. His healing drove him into a new purpose of coaching and guidance, and she was inspired to watch him turn his life into something he loved.

Marcus, 45 and always just a beat too chill, laughed mid-chew. "They hit me for haircuts weekly, like I'm not trying to run a business. And if I say no? Suddenly, I'm the 'absent uncle.'" He popped a grape in his mouth and leaned forward. "But let me post a pic with a fresh fit? Whole inbox lit." Marcus was a fantastic barber. He got his barber license at the age of 20. He knew he wanted to go to barber school right after high school. His mother ensured that no matter what they all did in life, they would complete high school and follow their dreams. And if they didn't have dreams, they'd find something productive and interesting to do. She loved that he wanted to become a barber and willingly helped him pay for school. He paid her back every dime before he turned 25. Marcus was a fantastic barber and kept his chair full daily. Even at the age of 22, he would be bringing in close to $1,000 per week.

He loved to do hair and was invested in cutting hair since he was young. He would chill in the barbershop, located right down the street from their old house on the south side, with the old heads, where he learned to play chess. He would also listen to their stories and learn about life. He even knew about shit he shouldn't have that would piss his mother off. Aseeka laughed, remembering her mother's face when he came home curious at 11 and asked her what happens when humans are in "doggy style?" Her mother marched to the barbershop and made them explain it to him right before her. Watching grown men try to tell a young boy what doggy style was in front of his mother was hilarious. They were a bit cautious around him after that but would warn him to keep his mouth shut about specific topics when he returned home.

Shanice, 47, owner of Slay'd by Shanice, rolled her eyes so hard her lashes fluttered. She was dressed in a cropped denim jacket, gold hoops, and nude heels like she'd stepped straight off the salon floor to the family table.

"Mmm, child, you lucky yours just want haircuts. Mine want lace fronts and loan money. And they got the nerve to call me 'the rich auntie.' Like I'm Oprah with a press comb." Aseeka remembered how Shanice used to do the hair on her Barbie dolls when they were younger. She was five years older than Aseeka and would often comb her hair if her mother was too busy to do it before school. She could replicate any hairstyle she had seen on TV or in an ad. Everyone would come to her and get their hair done. She fell in love with a dope boy who helped open her salon at 24. He was shot and killed shortly after, and he willed the salon to her. She went to cosmetology school out of high school.

Aseeka believed this also inspired Marcus to do hair. Shanice rented Marcus his first chair out of her shop. He worked there for a few years before the building next door became empty. Shanice and Marcus collaborated, and Marcus bought the building next door. Within a few years, they owned the Sinclair mini-mall on the Southside and set up a profitable operation. Everybody needed their hair done and needed to buy hair products! You could go to Slay'd, the salon, and get your hair done or to Creased and get a fresh cut. Next door to Creased was Sinclairs, the beauty supply store. They had all the hair products you could think of, clothes, shoes, and more selling out of there, and it was always packed, especially on the weekends. They had their shit together and helped Aseeka through law school if she needed it, which she often didn't, but because she was the baby, they would still visit and give her money just because. Her mother intentionally raised them as a tight group and ensured they always cared for one another.

Aseeka smirked, setting down her glass. "They only call me when their financial aid ain't hit yet.' Meanwhile, nobody says thank you or 'Happy Birthday,' but let me post a beach pic. They in the DMs like, 'Damn Auntie, you ballin.'"

Shanice cackled. "It's giving ATM with a side of guilt trip."

Anthony chuckled. "Man, look at us. Whole table of givers. It's amazing the things we do give, especially cause we understand the feeling of going without it, you know. We are the real MVPs."

"And low-key haters," Marcus added with a grin.

They laughed, that layered laughter only siblings know, where the jokes land, but the history of love, struggle, and happiness lingers beneath.

Then the air shifted, as it always did when Mama plotted something.

"I'm just saying," Shanice said, eyes narrowing, "Mama been talking about this 'big surprise' all week. Anybody got a guess?"

"Maybe she found Daddy's old life insurance policy," Marcus joked. "We are finally rich."

Anthony cut his eyes toward the hallway. "Watch it be some long-lost cousin or some DNA ancestry drama. Or maybe she is ready to retire?"

"Or a man," Shanice said, arching her brow. "I swear, if she brought one of her church crushes up here, I'm flipping this table."

Their mother was still an attractive woman. At 73, she stood 6'1", with long gray hair that she knew exactly how to curl or straighten, thanks to Shanice. Her pretty smile could light up a room, and her 200-pound body was fit as she believed in keeping herself healthy. She never lapsed on the family gym membership and still pays for it. She was a track star who ran hurdles, the 200, and the 400-meter dash back then. She was the state champion and a beast in every event she competed in, and that is where she met their father. She had her first child, Anthony, at 24, after she finished running track in college and pursued her education degree to become a teacher. Her mother loved education and was one of those children who would spend her time at school and use education to give back and stay out of the streets.

Aseeka knew her mother's body language; today, something seemed a bit off, like nervousness was coming from her.

Aseeka didn't say anything right away. Her eyes moved to the hallway, her chest just a little tighter than it had been a moment ago.

Then the doorbell rang.

Sharp. Loud. Too casual to carry what it held.

Their mother's voice floated from the hallway. "Y'all sit tight. I got it."

Marcus leaned back. "This it."

Anthony exhaled. "It better not be some pyramid scheme ambassador."

Shanice smirked. "Or a surprise vow renewal. I ain't wear the right bra for all that."

But Aseeka had gone still.

The door creaked open.

Footsteps.

A pause.

Their mother's voice was softer now. Controlled.

"Come in, baby. They're all here."

Then, his voice.

Rougher than she remembered, but still familiar enough to punch the air out of her lungs.

"Hey, kids."

No one moved.

No one laughed.

Aseeka felt her wine glass trembling before she even registered her hand shaking.

Their father had walked back into their lives.

After decades of absence, heartbreak, and unanswered questions.

Back into her mother's house.

Back into *their* house.

And there he was.

David Sinclair.

Her father.

Fresh out after 25 years of being locked up.

A profound silence came over the room as their mother scanned their faces, trying to read their reactions as she had done to her students and staff all these years. Her ability to read a room made her a fantastic principal, and her empathy helped her reach people. It was a skill and a gene she passed down to her children. And in this moment, she knew shit was about to hit the fan. He was sitting in his old recliner like nothing had changed. Like his sins hadn't rippled through all their lives.

His eyes softened when he saw her, but she didn't let him get past "Hi, baby girl" before turning away.

Monica's eyes darted around her children like she was trying to keep everyone in check. Sensing the uncomfortable silence, she stated, "Let's eat before the food gets cold." Hoping that the presence of food would help break the awkward ass silence.

Their father had served 25 years in prison for killing a man. They never really knew why, except it was about their mother. They never discussed it much, and if they brought it up, their mother would tell him, "he was protecting me." And that was the story they knew. When he was released, he kept his distance. He would often send a birthday card occasionally and call on holidays. He didn't want his children to see him locked up and begged their mother not to bring them up there. He especially didn't want his sons to see him caged like some animal. He was a very intelligent man and found God while he was in prison. He became a pastor and has been helping convicted felons turn their lives around through his church. Aseeka's mother made her promise not to go digging through his case file, and she kept that promise but always wondered what happened in the case. He had so much to share with them, but didn't know where to start.

Dinner started as always: loud, chaotic, plates passed like a relay race.

But Aseeka couldn't focus.

Every time her eyes drifted to her father, all she saw was that name in the file: Marcus Voss, deceased. David McGregor-Sinclair was convicted.

Her father's crime.

The gynecologist's brother.

The coincidence felt like a sick joke.

Halfway through dinner, Anthony casually mentioned her new case.

"Heard you pulled that Garvin case," he said, wiping his mouth. "Big one."

Aseeka's fork paused mid-air.

Her father's eyes flicked up.

"What's that?" David asked.

"Some doctor on trial. Sexual misconduct," Anthony replied casually.

Aseeka felt her father's stare heavy on her.

"You alright, baby girl?" David asked quietly.

They knew not to disrespect their father, or their mother would tear into them with no filter. She always spoke of him respectfully and ensured they knew the great genes he had handed them. He was an intellectual man who made a lot of bad choices. But he loved his family and would kill for them, and he did. They just didn't know everything. Over time, they stopped wondering and moved on with life, but it was often the elephant in the room. Aseeka pondered if that was why she gravitated towards a law career, but never said much about it because she couldn't stomach giving him credit for her success.

She looked at him, her stomach twisting, rage and confusion simmering beneath her skin.

"Fine," she lied, cutting into her food like it had done something to her.

He decided not to push the issue, but deep down inside, he knew he'd have to tell her everything. He'd reach out at another time to have that conversation.

The dinner plates mainly sat untouched. Forks pushed food around like no one had the stomach for what they'd just swallowed. The house was too quiet now; there was no laughter or teasing, just the sound of a man trying to breathe.

Anthony sat at the far end of the table, arms folded, eyes hard. Marcus leaned back, tapping the side of his glass, jaw tight. Shanice wiped the same spot on her napkin for the third time. And Aseeka, seated across from the man who used to be her father, looked at him like she didn't know which version was before her.

Their mother had gone to the kitchen. She knew this had to happen. She had been preparing for this moment.

"Alright," Anthony said, voice deep and even. "Let's stop pretending we're at some surprise family reunion. You got our attention. Now say what you came here to say."

Anthony had become the man of the house after his father's incarceration. He honored that position as protector and wore it like a badge of honor. Of course, he would kick it off.

Their father, Charles Sinclair, looked older, but something in his eyes still carried the weight of the man who used to tuck them in at night. His hands trembled as he laid his napkin on the table.

"I didn't leave y'all because I didn't love you," he began, voice already breaking. "I left because I couldn't stand the idea of you seeing me in a prison jumpsuit. I didn't want your memory of me being... that."

Marcus cut in, sharp. "Then you should've said goodbye like a man. Instead, you just disappeared. Left Ma to pick up the pieces."

"I didn't have a choice!" David snapped, then immediately dropped his voice. "I had to protect her. I had to protect this family."

Shanice leaned in, eyes wet but steady. "From what, Daddy? From yourself?"

"No," he said, shaking his head. "From *him*."

The table went still.

David looked at each of his children, the words heavy in his mouth.

"His name was Marcus Voss. He'd been stalking your mother for weeks. Leaving notes on her windshield. Calling the house. Watching her from the street. You remember that night I came in bleeding and told y'all it was just a fall?"

They nodded slowly.

"That was from him. He jumped me behind the church one night. Said if she didn't stop rejecting him, he was gonna hurt her, or worse. I tried to go to the police, but he was smart. Covered his tracks. Knew people. He was like a hood celebrity."

His voice cracked now. His eyes were glassy.

"One night, I caught him outside the house. He had a weapon. I snapped. I wasn't trying to be a hero. I just ... I wasn't gonna let him touch her. Not on my watch."

Silence.

"I killed him."

David could still hear the bullet from his gun going off as her emptied the clip in Marcus's body.

The words thudded against the walls like a storm had entered the room.

David continued. "They gave me 25 years. I served all 25. Even though I had no priors. But I guess that is the cost of killing someone in broad daylight. I spent the first few trying to forgive myself. I spent the rest trying to figure out how I'd ever face you again."

Anthony exhaled hard, eyes closed, fists clenched. "And for a year after you got out? Still nothing?"

"I had to go through the halfway house," David said. "They monitored everything. Then, I started preaching again at a small church on the West Side. I started helping ex-cons get clean and back on their feet. I wanted to walk back into your lives, a man you could respect. Not a project. Not a mess. I also had to ensure his people wouldn't come after y'all."

Aseeka looked down, her voice quieter than usual. "We thought you were dead. I thought … you just didn't care."

"I never stopped caring," David whispered, eyes locked on hers. "Not for one second."

Marcus set his fork down with a thud. "Look. I'm not about to sit here and act like I'm okay. I missed you, and I hated you at the same time. I watched Ma cry at night, thinking we didn't see. I carried that. Every damn day."

Anthony nodded. "Same. I had to be the man of the house before I even knew what manhood was. I had to grow up overnight. So yeah, we are grown now. But that little inner child in me? He's still waiting for his dad to show up."

Shanice's voice cracked as she spoke. "I raised those boys with Mama. And I buried every memory of you like it was easier than feeling the hole you left behind."

They were hurt.

But they weren't cruel.

Anthony looked at his father, his jaw still tight. "Out of respect for Mama, we won't disrespect you. But forgiveness? That's gon' take time."

David nodded, tears streaming freely down his cheeks. "That's all I ask. Time."

Aseeka finally stood, walking to the kitchen and returning with a fresh plate. She set it in front of him without a word. The gesture wasn't forgiveness. Not yet.

But it was something.

"Eat," she said softly. "You're here now."

And for the first time in years, David Sinclair ate dinner with all his children at the table.

Not as a ghost.

But as a man.

Dinner moved on.

Jokes, teasing, side-eyes.
But Aseeka couldn't hear any of it.

Her father's voice from years ago echoed in her head:

Some things you gotta carry alone.

She finally understood what he meant.

And she hated him for it.

Chapter 16: Pre-flight Confessions

Tasha had been talking about this damn party for weeks.

She texted Tasha and sent her a screenshot of the confirmation. Then Tasha called her enthusiastically and began to plan everything from outfits to plane rides to hotel stays. It was like they were in college all over again; shit was about to be lit! She promised to meet her for lunch so they could discuss it and plan accordingly. Aseeka needed to know every logistical thing; it was her way of maintaining control.

The sun poured over the rooftop patio like warm honey, kissing Aseeka's bare shoulders as she adjusted her sunglasses and leaned back into the cushion of her chair. The Chicago skyline shimmered behind them, but all she could focus on was Tasha, legs crossed, mimosa in hand, lip gloss glistening, and that mischievous smirk she always wore when she was up to something.

"I still can't believe I said yes to this shit," Aseeka said, sipping on her elderflower spritz. "A sex club opening, Tasha? In LA? With your man flying us out like a damn rap video?"

Tasha laughed, full-bodied and unapologetic. "Correction: *exclusive* adult club. Upscale. Black-owned. Byron's pulling out all the stops. Private jet, penthouse at The W, VIP section overlooking the dance floor. You deserve a little scandal, Judge Sinclair."

Aseeka raised an eyebrow. "Mhm. And what exactly happens at this club? Like ... folks just out here raw-dogging on velvet couches?"

Tasha grinned. "Girl, no. It's classy. Think ... eyes-wide-shut meets Beyoncé visuals. Consent everywhere. Kinks catered to. Safe spaces. Baskets of condoms, for both ya dick or ya pussy, and the rooms? Soundproof. Mirror ceilings. High-thread-count sheets. You can watch, participate, or sip champagne and act judgmental in a corner."

Aseeka choked on her drink, laughing. "So, it's giving high-end hoe behavior."

"Exactly. With hors d'oeuvres."

They both cackled.

Then Aseeka's voice dropped, curiosity getting the best of her. "And this drug? Crave? You gonna debut it at the party?"

Tasha leaned in, eyes glittering. "Soft launch, baby. Just a lil sample station. Nothing wild. Just ... a taste. Literally."

"And it really works?"

"Girl. It's like your body starts talking to you in moans. You feel warm, sensitive, and open. It's like legal ecstasy. For women, it boosts natural lubrication and heightens sensitivity. For men, it enhances blood flow and turns everything *on*."

Aseeka gave her a knowing look. "And I helped fund this freaky little science experiment."

"You did. And you're gonna thank me when you finally stop clenching your thighs and let loose for once."

Aseeka snorted. "Please. I'm not the prude you think I am."

Tasha tilted her head, lips curling into something softer. "I don't think you're a prude. I just think ... you're used to being in control. Crave doesn't take that from you; it just reminds you that pleasure is power, too."

There was something in her voice, low and loaded. A flicker passed between them. A pause that stretched just long enough to mean something.

Aseeka sipped her drink to break the moment. "Even though the drug is not FDA approved yet?

Tasha spoke confidently, "It passed the first round of approval. We're just waiting on the next, and I think we'll be fine. Plus, everyone will sign a disclaimer, understanding the risk if they indulge. We are transparent about it not being FDA-approved yet, but the clinical trials have been going well!

Aseeka felt a bit of comfort but was still unsettled, so she decided not to press the issue about Crave. "You sure Byron's cool with all this?"

"Oh, he's *thrilled.* He's obsessed with the idea of you coming."

Aseeka blinked. "Wait ... what?"

Tasha waved it off with a casual shrug. "Relax. He respects you. He's just excited. You're smart, sexy, and powerful. Of course, he's curious."

"Mmhmm," Aseeka murmured, narrowing her eyes. "And what about you?"

Aseeka wasn't stupid; she knew Tasha was in love with Byron. And even though she'd never sleep with him, she didn't want any resentment between them.

Tasha didn't flinch. Just smiled slowly and licked the mimosa foam off her lip. "I stay curious."

Their laughter returned, but it was thicker now, charged, wrapped in secrets they weren't ready to unwrap. Not yet.

Aseeka sat back and looked at the sky, "so when does this plane leave?"

Tasha smirked, "Saturday at 6 a.m., so we have time to get settled and for the festivities on Saturday."

Aseeka was excited; she had taken the entire weekend off, including Friday; she needed a fucking vacation, especially before the start of this damn trial.

And neither of them was ready for just how wild things were about to get.

"A grown folks' party," she called it, lips curling around her wine glass like she was selling temptation itself.

Aseeka had laughed it off at first and called her crazy, but tonight?

 After the file. After the family dinner. After the stress of it all.

She needed something reckless. She was ready for the moment, but first, she had a decision to make regarding this damn case. She knew she had to talk to her father but wasn't ready. She'd worry about that when they returned on Sunday.

For now, it was time to unwind in the wildest way possible.

Chapter 17: The Land of Angels and Desire

The jet cut through the clouds like it had somewhere sexy to be.

Inside, it was less "airplane" and more "floating VIP lounge." Champagne was chilled in gold-rimmed flutes, the leather seats were soft as sin, and Aseeka had kicked off her heels two hours ago, laughing with Tasha between fruit bites and flirtation.

Tasha wore a cream, two-piece lounge set that hugged her hips like love letters. She sprawled across the couch with her silk bonnet still tied, scrolling through her phone and occasionally side-eyeing Aseeka with a grin that meant *she was texting Byron about her.*

Aseeka, still in soft glam and mocha-colored travel sweats, stretched and looked out the window at the California coastline, beginning to peek through the clouds.

"You know," she said, sipping the last of her champagne, "I thought you were exaggerating with all this private jet talk. But I'm not going back to O'Hare after this."

Tasha laughed. "Girl, once you fly like this, TSA is dead to you."

The pilot's voice came on soft and smooth. "Ladies, we're beginning our descent into Los Angeles. Estimated ground time: 15 minutes. Your driver will be waiting on the tarmac."

Tasha sat up, already pulling off her bonnet and fluffing her curls. "Showtime."

"Wait," Aseeka said, adjusting her lip gloss in a compact mirror. "Are we going straight to the hotel, or do we get to breathe and eat first? You know I have to have my In-N-Out!"

Tasha smirked. "Straight to the penthouse, baby. Byron pulled strings to get us the top floor at the W. Balcony view. Two bedrooms. A minibar with an actual top shelf. And a personal concierge."

Aseeka raised a brow. "So ... he's really tryna impress."

"You have *no* idea."

The wheels hit the runway with a soft thud, and moments later, the cabin doors opened to warm LA air, and a black Escalade waited just off the tarmac, engine running.

The driver stepped out in all black, holding a tablet with their name already glowing on the screen.

"Ms. Sinclair. Ms. James. Welcome to Los Angeles."

Tasha winked at Aseeka as they walked toward the SUV. "Told you. We're not in Chicago anymore."

Inside the car, the seats were chilled, the scent was the new car smell and vanilla, and a custom playlist of R&B hits played softly as the skyline came into view.

As they rode through downtown, the vibe shifted. The sun was setting like it knew something. And Aseeka, looking out the window at the palm trees swaying in rhythm, couldn't shake the feeling that something was about to happen.

Something she hadn't planned for.

Something she might want.

Beside her, Tasha leaned in closer, her voice low, teasing.

"You ready for tonight?"

Aseeka didn't answer immediately. She smiled, biting her bottom lip just a little.

"Do I have a choice? If not, I think I'm about to be."

The black Escalade curved up the palm-lined driveway of the W Hotel Hollywood like it knew it was carrying VIPs. The valets moved like choreography; one opened Tasha's door with a "Welcome, Ms. James," and another swooped in to grab their designer luggage before either could lift a finger.

The lobby was pure seduction, prefacing the feeling the night had in store. Dim lighting, marble floors, and a perfume in the air that smelled like black card energy and unspoken secrets. Guests in designer fits and oversized sunglasses walked past like they were headed to castings, photo shoots, sex parties ... or all three.

Aseeka paused at the front desk, letting it all sink in.

"Y'all not playing," she whispered to Tasha.

Tasha grinned, slipping the concierge a tip with a wink. "Told you. Byron doesn't do basic."

The elevator ride to the penthouse was silent but thick with energy. Tasha watched Aseeka in the mirrored walls, her curves, confidence, and curiosity. Byron wasn't the only one craving a taste.

Ding.

The elevator doors opened into a private vestibule. No hallway. Just Suite 2801.

Their concierge unlocked the door and stepped back, letting the women walk into a space that felt more like a magazine spread than a hotel room.

The penthouse was breathtaking.

Glass walls looked out over all of Los Angeles, downtown, the hills, and even a sliver of the ocean if you stood just right. The sun was low, spilling gold into the living area where velvet couches and black marble tables sat under a chandelier of dripping glass.

To the left, a chef's kitchen with a stocked wine fridge and curated snacks. To the right are two bedrooms, each with a California king bed, plush throws, mood lighting, and blackout curtains for the nights that turned into mornings.

The main bath had a rainfall shower, a soaking tub with jets, and a wall mirror that slid open to reveal a flat-screen and Bluetooth sound.

But the best part?

The balcony.

Huge. Private. It was lined with planters, lanterns, and a curved sectional built for lounging, talking … or anything else the night brought.

Tasha walked in as if she owned it, kicking off her heels and flopping onto the living room couch. "God, I love being rich-adjacent."

Aseeka stood at the glass, sipping in the skyline like wine. "This is unreal."

Tasha stretched. "Byron left a few gifts in your room."

Aseeka turned slowly. "What kind of gifts?"

"Designer lingerie. Champagne. A little note that says, 'I can't wait to see you tonight.'"

Aseeka blinked. "Wait. He left it *for me*?"

Tasha stood now, walking over with that knowing little grin. "You're the guest of honor, babe. Might as well enjoy the perks."

Aseeka narrowed her eyes, half-joking, half-alarmed. "Is this a seduction setup?"

Tasha just shrugged and walked toward her own bedroom. "Depends. You planning to be seduced?"

The door clicked behind her.

Aseeka stood in the silence, heartbeat doing a soft little drumroll behind her ribs.

She looked back at the view.

Then, back at the bedroom door.

The bedroom smelled like sandalwood and rose water, soft and heady. On the velvet bench at the foot of the bed sat a matte black gift box, thick satin ribbon tied in a perfect knot. A crisp envelope rested on top, her name handwritten in clean, confident strokes.

"Aseeka."

She opened the note slowly.

> *"For the kind of night your body still*
> *remembers in the morning.*
> *Wear this. Or don't. Either way, I'll be*
> *watching.*
> *– B"*

Her lips curled into something between curiosity and danger. She was attracted to Byron, and deep down, she was intrigued, but was trying her best to fight the urge that nested deep inside her soul. She wrestled between the discomfort and the yearning she had to feel more. She loved Damon and was very sexually satisfied with him, but it always felt as if something was missing.

Inside the box, nestled in layers of black tissue paper, was a piece of art disguised as lingerie: a sheer black bodysuit that left just enough to the imagination but everything to the senses. The cups were trimmed in scalloped lace with delicate underwires that lifted rather than covered. Gold hardware glinted at the straps, adjustable and soft, and the hips were cut high to frame her body like poetry.

Beside it, a pair of strappy black stilettos, the kind with red bottoms and cruelty written in the arch, rested next to a silky floor-length robe with a thigh-high slit and sleeves that whispered when they moved.

Aseeka took a deep breath.

She hadn't worn anything like this in a long time, not because she couldn't, but because she hadn't *needed* to. She wore power on the bench, robe, and gavel. But tonight? Power would come wrapped in lace.

She laid the bodysuit across the bed, then moved to her open suitcase and pulled out her own piece: a black satin corset dress, boned for structure but soft enough to cling. High slit. Off-shoulder neckline. And a choker necklace she hadn't worn since a night she still couldn't talk about.

She glanced again at the note as she stepped toward the bathroom to begin getting ready.

She wasn't sure if she'd wear it.

But she *was* sure the night was going to remember her.

And for the first time in a long time, she wondered what it would feel like to say *yes*.

Chapter 18: Fuck!

Two hours after arriving, the penthouse transformed into a backstage glam suite. Byron had sent a celebrity makeup artist and a personal hair stylist to their room, no questions asked. Hair curled, laid, or pinned to perfection. Faces beat in soft mattes and shimmers that kissed their cheekbones and made their eyes smolder. Tasha's lips were a glossy nude; Aseeka's were a deep wine red, danger in a tube.

When they were finally alone again, stepping in front of the full-length mirror, they didn't speak at first.

They just stared.

Two goddesses.

Undeniable. Flawless. Ready.

Aseeka's dress was a midnight black corset gown, sculpted like it had been sewn onto her. The satin clung to her hips, dipped low off her shoulders, and wrapped her curves like it had secrets to keep. The neckline plunged just enough to tease, her breasts lifted by the built-in boning, kissed with a highlighter. A thigh-high slit revealed her toned leg, and the black strappy stilettos wrapped around her ankles like restraints she didn't plan to escape.

Her jewelry was minimal, a single diamond choker glittered like it knew her name, and a cuff bracelet etched with ancient African script. Her pixie cut was curled perfectly, and the front curls dangled like vines over her forehead, marking sacred territory.

She looked ... *untouchable*. And yet, every inch of her body said *try me*.

Tasha, on the other hand, wore red like she invented it.

A deep cherry latex catsuit molded to her body like a second skin. The neckline dipped into a sharp V between her breasts, and the back was almost entirely exposed, held together by two crisscrossed straps that barely held on. Her hips were hugged tight, and the outfit zipped from waist to navel, offering easy access she pretended not to notice.

Her heels were firetruck red stilettos, pointed toes, gold accents at the heel, and just disrespectful in height. Her hair was slicked back into a braided ponytail that swung like punctuation every time she turned.

As she turned to Aseeka, she smiled slowly. "You ready?"

Aseeka smirked, adjusting her strap. "I was born ready. But now? I'm dangerous."

They stepped out of the suite together, every head in the hallway turning as the elevator doors closed behind them.
The city didn't know what was coming.
But Climax would never forget them.

The private club was discreet, downtown, on the top floor, with no signs on the door. You had to know someone to get in.

Once the Escalade dropped them off, they walked down a black carpet that led to the private entrance. Inside, the lights were low, the music was velvet and bass, and the air hummed with sex.

Tasha approached the tall, chiseled-faced doorman and pulled out her black envelope. The guard scanned the gold ticket, and once the scanner beeped, the tall black door behind him automatically opened.

As soon as the door opened, the guard gestured for them to pass through, and Aseeka felt a rush of adrenaline. She didn't know what she was about to see, but she was ready. They stood in a blank room, waiting to see what would come next. The red lights colored the tall white walls. The chandelier hung from the ceiling like a frozen moment mid-swoon, a cascade of hand-blown glass droplets suspended in layers that shimmered with every shift of light. Each teardrop caught the glow and bent it into something golden like the room was exhaling glamour. Its frame was black iron, slender and coiled like calligraphy, holding the weight of beauty and silence.

From below, light was dripping from heaven, soft, moody, and hypnotic. Shadows danced on the walls, swaying with the flicker of the bulbs, casting lace-like patterns that made even stillness feel alive.

It didn't just light the room through the red bulbs; it watched over it, commanding presence without saying a word.

Aseeka stared at it for a few seconds, mesmerized, then began scanning the room, trying to locate an entrance.

Out of nowhere, a door you could not see without opening came out of a wall. A tall Pam Greer-looking woman came out. She was dressed in a long, red, sheer dress. Her perfect size DD breast implants sat up on her chest with effortless vigor. She stood about 6'1" in her four-inch heels and walked toward them like a model on a runway. She handed them small red silk bags with the word Climax written in gold Calligraphy font on the front. Inside the bag, there was a packet with a Crave pill with a small disclaimer attached to it, a small bottle of Moët & Chandon Champagne, a black satin blindfold, VIP wristbands, stickers, lubricants, and condoms of all different flavors. She instructed them to put one of the color-coded stickers on their wristbands.

The stickers read "open, spectator, or active participant and each role had an explanation next to it. Aseeka decided to go with open, which meant asking me if I was interested, and we'll take it from there. The wristband had ASK FOR CONSENT on it to remind everyone that this was a safe sexual space. Byron didn't play about that shit, he'd kick you out in a heartbeat and have security drag you to the alley, and you better hope you'd ever be seen again if you violated the consent clause. Everyone had to read and agree to it online before receiving the event location. The woman waited for them to put on their badges and sternly said, "I'll need both of your phones. They will be stored in a locker and associated with the numbers on your wristband. You can collect them from the concierge desk inside this wall when the party ends, or you decide to leave. Once they handed over their phones, she gestured for them to follow her without saying a word as they walked through the entrance to the wall.

As they entered the opening, they heard the woman's deep, sensual voice linger behind them, "Welcome to Climax. This will be a night to remember." She walked over to a small desk, handed them to the man standing behind her, and directed him to place them in one of the small lockers on the wall behind him. There were hundreds of tiny lockers, and many of them were closed and locked. Aseeka didn't mind; it comforted her that no one was allowed to take pictures.

Once their wrist bands were scanned to match their lockers, they walked over to look at the floor below them and the festivities. They stood on the club's upper level overlooking the dancefloor and the stage.. In the middle of the floor was the stage where the new famous neo soul artist Syrah, who focused on sexually sensual music, perfect for this event, was playing. Her voice echoed through the speakers, and her dancers surrounded the stage. Women, men, and nonbinary people of different sizes and shades of melanin were moving their bodies to the music on the stage. They were dressed in various types of lingerie and wearing masquerade ball masks in baskets by the entrance. Their bodies moved effortlessly alongside the music, and the choreography was screaming seduction and liberation. Which is what her music was all about. Her beautiful chocolate skin and blonde curly afro hair bounced to the baseline. Aseeka watched in awe as it was all so sexy.

Admiring Byron's vision and execution of such a fantastic venue and night. She had to admit, she was impressed.

Aseeka grabbed a classic Black mask and immediately put it on. Tasha grabbed a green and red one to match her outfit.

Around the club, they could see people in masks, silk robes, and people wearing little to nothing else drifting from room to room like shadows.

Tasha squeezed her hand. "You good?"

Aseeka nodded, jaw tight. "Let's see what all the fuss is about." They observed from the top floor and watched all the people wearing everything from birthday suits to robes to lingerie dancing and gyrating all over each other on the dance floor. Cleaners were walking around picking up empty packages of Crave off the floor and keeping the whole place sanitized throughout the night.

A server approached them with a tray of champagne glasses and shots of top-shelf liquor. Aseeka grabbed a champagne glass, and Tasha grabbed a shot of Patron. The server also had breath mints ready for anyone who needed them. Tasha pulled the Crave pill out of her bag and showed it to Aseeka, prompting her to grab hers.

Tasha ripped open the package and said, "Take it now; it takes about 15-20 minutes to kick in; the alcohol will help it kick in faster."

Aseeka studied the little pink pill before taking it; she could feel a bit of hesitancy since she had never taken any kind of illegal drugs before, but she decided to let go. She watched Tasha take hers along with the entire shot of tequila. She followed suit and took the pill, followed by the entire flute of champagne.

Tasha swayed back and forth seductively and cheered enthusiastically as she watched her friend take her creation. She knew it would help her loosen up and make the night more interesting.

They walked around the club for 10 minutes, taking moments to stop and dance and then resume looking for Byron, but couldn't find him. Tasha stopped to greet the stars she had invited to the party. She was a beautiful, energetic, funny, and always smiling socialite. She introduced Aseeka to everyone she greeted or those who greeted her. Everyone from professional ball players to NFL players and music artists was there. Legends were in the building, staring at other people as if they were ready to be consumed by sexual pleasure. After about 20 minutes of socializing, they found Byron. He was standing in the upstairs office window, looking down at everybody from the big-ass window located above the dance floor. He found Tasha and motioned for her to give him 10 minutes; he was wrapping up.

Just as Aseeka was about to say something about her pill not having any effect, she felt a rise in temperature in her body. She felt everything start to slow down. She started staring at her hand, holding onto the glass of champagne she was babysitting. The glass felt colder, harder, and wetter as the precipitation had built up around it. She didn't notice that her free hand was now caressing the glass. She looked up and saw Tasha smiling, licking her shot glass.

Tasha paused for a minute and looked at Aseeka with her big beautiful ass smile and said enthusiastically, "That shit starting to kick in, isn't it?"

Aseeka just nodded. She went to open her mouth to say something, but the intensity from her, the feeling of her lips being pressed together, was starting to cause her pussy lips to pulsate. Every feeling felt more intense; she could even feel the arch of her feet pressing deeply against her heels. She was sitting in sexual stillness and focusing on all the naked and half-naked people walking around free as fuck, not caring what anyone thought. She could feel herself getting emotional as she gazed deeply at thicker bodies, thin bodies, big dicks, little dicks, And everything in between. They didn't want to keep dancing, and Tasha was on the hunt for Byron.

So, they decided to try the private rooms. Only people with VIP wristbands were allowed.

Tasha, realizing her friend was in a trance after trying the pill for the first time, looked at her and said, "Let's find a place to sit."

They walked along the wall of the hallway, where there were numerous black and gold doors. Tasha opened a door on the right, and they looked in to find a man watching a woman dance behind a glass window. It was a peep show happening in real time. The woman had her titties pressed against the window while her hips swerved to slow, seductive music. The man occasionally placed gold coins in a slot beneath the window and instructed her on what to do. The woman was completely naked, with a pussy covered in black pubic hair, and her light skin was glowing under the green seductive light she was dancing under. She wore a mask to protect her identity as the man directed her to put her fingers in her pussy and moan his name. He didn't even notice the two women standing in the doorway behind him. He was mesmerized by the show and in complete awe of this beautiful, full-figured, curly-haired woman dancing for him. He sat on a stool in silk boxers, wearing a gold and black mask to match his outfit, but he seemed familiar to Aseeka. She couldn't see his face, but she knew that voice from somewhere; as he took his right hand and covered it in line from the grab bag, they knew it was their time to stop spectating. Tasha closed the door and didn't say a word to each other; they just moved on to find a place to sit.

They came to another room, and Tasha opened the door and found a man sitting in a white king's chair. And a small petite woman with long black straight hair bouncing up and down viciously on his enormous dick. Aseeka instantly felt her pussy growing wetter and wetter as she watched the woman's voluptuous ass bounce up and down on the man. Her olive complexion was perspiring from the work she was putting in, and no telling how long they had been there. The man had his head leaned back with his hands gripping her hips, helping to guide her up and down. The woman feeling eyes on her, looked over her left shoulder and glanced at Aseeka, "Come join us; you can sit on his face while I focus on his dick."

Before Aseeka could answer, Tasha answered for her, "No, thank you, we have our own private party to attend, but you do you boo! Keep working his ass!"

They heard the man laugh out loud as Tasha closed the door. Still holding on to Aseeka's hand like the protective friend that she was, they finally came to an empty room. They walked into this room, and the only thing in it looked like a massage bed covered in plush fur, with candles lit all along the wall. A large canopy draping from the ceiling circled around the massage bed, leaving space for people to walk through it and around it. In the corner was a red and black queen chair with a black leather whip and a paddle hanging from the top.

Aseeka felt her knees get weak and finally found the strength to speak after the pill had started to take full effect throughout her body. Her nipples were hard, her pussy was wet and throbbing, and she felt ready for anything. As she walked over to the queen chair, still in a bit of a trance, she heard the door to the room open and shut. She looked up to see Byron standing there in his black silk robe that was wide open, showing off his chiseled Mandingo Warrior-looking body, his black silk shorts hugging his muscular thighs, and his big ass dick poking out of the slit of his boxer shorts. He wore a gold masquerade mask with black feathers hanging off the sides. He walked through the canopy and stood over the massage bed. The dim lighting from the room was setting the seductive tone. Aseeka had to admit his presence turned her on, but she tried to ignore the feeling. Byron was Tasha's man; she could never! Or could she? As she sat in the chair and prepared to watch the show, she thought only he and Tasha were about to put on.

He finally spoke, his deep ass voice running through Aseeka's ears, "Come here, Tasha; I've been waiting for your sexy asses all night."

Tasha ensured Aseeka was in the chair before she headed over to Byron, who was standing like a fierce soldier next to the massage bed. He grabbed one of the pillows off the bed and dropped it on the ground in front of him. Tasha already knew what time it was; she walked up and passionately kissed him in the mouth, then dropped to her knees on top of the pillow below him. She immediately stuck out her tongue and circled the top of his dick gently. She made three circles before sucking the head entirely in her mouth. Byron gently placed his hand on her head as he watched Aseeka sit in the chair and observe.

Aseeka could feel herself becoming more and more turned on. She thought to herself, " Girl, what the fuck are you doing? Get up and get out of here!" Her mind was saying one thing, but it was as if her body couldn't move. She knew leaving was probably a good idea, but she couldn't muster the strength to excite the space. It was like she had become connected to it; the leather from the chair felt welcoming. She literally could not move. She was on a journey and wanted to watch the show as she could hear the sounds of Byron's dick thrusting in and out of Tasha's mouth. The sounds of his moans were turning her on.

So, she obliged her body and decided to let go for once. So, she slowly sat back in the chair, pulled the top of her dress down, and began pinching her nipples. After she had had enough of her nipples, she took one hand and put it in her panties and started to rub on her clit. She let out a moan as the enhancement from Crave heightened her senses, and she was wetter than she ever remembered. She kept her eyes on Byron, who tapped Tasha on the shoulder, prompting her to stop. Tasha looked up at him as he gestured for her to hold on, and he slowly started to make his way to Aseeka. He grabbed the other pillow from the massage bed and held on to it as he walked towards her. Clutching it like it was some kind of trophy. Aseeka was fully mesmerized and couldn't help herself; she was in full sexual ecstasy.

Byron dropped the pillow down in front of Aseeka. She couldn't take her eyes off his dick that was six inches from her face. He leaned in and gently started to suck on her right nipple and then slowly slid his tongue across her chest and took her left nipple in his mouth. The feeling of his warm tongue on her nipples ran through her body like a burst of adrenaline. He repeated this for about two minutes as he slowly gripped her panties. He pulled her toward him by her hips and, without notice, ripped her panties off. He smelled them and smiled as he placed them in the pocket of his robe. He looked dead in her eyes and smiled, "You don't know how long I've waited for this moment." He then spread her legs and placed each one over the arm of the seat. He slowly moved his tongue to her fully exposed pussy while never breaking eye contact. And before she could respond, he was nose deep in her pussy. Never before had she contemplated such a moment between her and Byron; she didn't expect it, but she wasn't disappointed.

In between slurps, Byron talked about how wet she was; he kissed her thighs and then went right back to devouring her. Within a matter of minutes, she could feel her body ready to erupt. The feeling of his wet tongue on her pussy was making her back arch and her lower body shake. He knew what the fuck he was doing. She was so lost in the amount of pleasure she was receiving from Byron she forgot about Tasha, who was now ass naked in the massage bed watching the show while she masturbated.

Aseeka decided to focus her attention on Byron because she knew she was about to cum. As she felt her body jerking, she felt a quick rush of excitement as Byron lifted her up off the chart completely and let her cum all over his face. She shivered as her pussy juices dripped down his face. Tasha climbed down off the table as she saw them moving towards her. And he slowly walked her over to the massage table and laid her down flat on her back. He positioned her so her head hung over the table's end. She lay there hornier than she had ever felt and entirely submissive for the seduction that was taking place.

Byron walked around the table and stood over her, smiling from ear to ear, her pussy juices still on his face. He slowly pressed the top of his dick against her lips until she opened her mouth and committed to taking it into her mouth. She was sucking it slowly and effortlessly. His dick was just a little bigger than Damon's but she was willing to take on the challenge. She had never felt so much pleasure taking dick in her mouth, and the sounds of his moans turned her on.

And out of nowhere, she felt her legs spread open at the other end of the table. She suddenly felt another warm tongue sliding down between her legs. The Crave pill had completely kicked in, and she could tell it was in full effect. Byron pulled his dick out of her mouth long enough for her to lift her head up and see Tasha between her legs. She wasn't as good as Byron, and Aseeka wasn't into women. She had tried it once in college, but it wasn't her thing. She was horny as fuck, but not enough to fuck with Tasha! She immediately reached down and pushed Tasha's head up and said loudly, "No, don't I'm not into that." Tasha looked at her friend but understood.

Walking around the table, Byron immediately grabbed Tasha by the chin, kissed her in the mouth, and said confidently, "No means no."

He then pointed to the chair so she could have a seat. And turned his focus back to Aseeka. Tasha was disappointed but understood and respected when she grabbed her clothes off the floor and left the room to find another group to join.

Meanwhile, Byron pushed Aseeka back down entirely on the table and spread her legs widely. Gripping both legs by the bottom of her knees, he slowly inserted his dick in her. Aseeka moaned out loudly as the feeling in her body felt heightened by the penetration. She could feel every vein of his dick slamming in and out of her pussy walls. Byron was staring intensely into her eyes as he spoke, "That dick feels good to you, doesn't it? Take that shit." He was speaking in between moans as he started to thrust his dick in and out of her harder and harder, and she screamed louder and louder.

He was also moaning as the Crave pill had also started to reach a climactic point in his body. The wetness of her pussy was driving him wild. He didn't want the moment to end. He had often daydreamed about it, and it was even better than he imagined. He paused, pulled his dick out, ready to change positions, and effortlessly flipped her over. He grabbed a pillow off the ground and placed it under her belly to help arch her ass in the air. He gave her another pillow and said cockily, "Bite that if the shit gets too real for you."

He climbed up behind her on the table and rammed his dick back into her pussy hole that was completely exposed and protruding in the air underneath her ass cheeks. He immediately started to stroke her deeply, intensely in a way that she had never felt before. He enjoyed the sound of her ass cheeks clapping against his dick as he fucked her so intensely that she was now digging her nails into the pillow. He felt a sense of accomplishment come over him as he listened to her moans.

Aseeka couldn't believe how good Byron's dick felt. She didn't know if it was the pill or if he was just that good with his dick. He laid on top of her so that she couldn't move and continued pounding her little tight pussy. He had now put her in a position where her body was completely stretched out, and she could feel his sweaty, chiseled body lying on her backside. He was in control, and she was being submissive to his needs. But something came over Aseeka, and she was ready to take back control.

She said softly in between the sounds of her ass cheeks clapping against Byron, "Please let me get on top." And he quickly obliged her request. He sat up and pulled his dick out as they switched positions. Aseeka then pushed him down on his back as she saw his eyes light up excitedly. She quickly straddled his hips and slowly sat down on his hard-ass dick. She had been practicing her Kegels and was ready to put them to work. She began bouncing her hips up and down slowly at first, and the more she heard him moan, the more she sped up. The feeling of his dick sliding in and out of her was turning her on in a way that she hadn't ever felt. Byron reached up and grabbed one of her titties in each hand and squeezed them gently. A sudden rush of pleasure grew over her body as she took her right hand and wrapped it as best as she could around his thick ass neck. She could feel him breathing and swallowing, which heightened the experience for her even more. She gripped his neck just enough not to hurt him but to send him crying out in pleasure. She was now in control, and she loved every minute of it. She thought, "I bet his muthafuckin toes are curling right now." As she heard his moans, she also felt another rush of undeniable ecstasy race through her body; she was about to come again. She smirked as Byron screamed in a high-pitched voice, "I'm cummin!" She was also about to climax, and as soon as she bounced one last time, she lifted her hips and felt cum rushing out of her pussy. Byron had also exploded, and a waterfall of cum came rushing out of his dick precisely at the same time that she climaxed. She collapsed on Byron as she felt his cum shooting out of his dick and dripping down her stomach. She lay there for a second as she felt his warm hands gripping her ass cheeks. She had just had some of the best sex of her life, and Tasha's new invention enhanced it, making the sex mind-blowing.

After a minute, she climbed off Byron and said nothing to him. She picked her dress up off the wall and fixed the mask on her face. She looked over and saw a small table with a pile of black silk robes. She grabbed one and put it on, hoping to find a shower somewhere in the club. She turned to Byron, who was trying his best to find his footing as his knees had grown weak, "Are there showers here?"

"Yeah, the private VIP ones are down the hall to the left, with blue doors. I need one, too; want me to join you?"

Aseeka, still high from the Crave, looked at him, and her eyes were still sparkling. "No, I'm good. Thanks, though." She walked out of the room.

The bass of the music still throbbed behind her ribcage as she moved down the private corridor. Her heels were in her hand now, bare feet padded against the cool tiles of Climax's floor, where the private rooms curved around the dancefloor like a voyeur's halo. The hallway was lit in soft amber, flickering low like candlelight, and each door she passed hummed with secrets.

She turned the corner and saw it, a sleek black door marked "Private Suite: Spa Use Only."

Unlocked.

She pushed it open.

The air inside was thick with eucalyptus and something floral, almost sacred. The room was tiled in matte obsidian and deep gray marble, walls glistening from steam. A single, wide rainfall shower stood in the center behind a curved frosted glass divider. A gold bench rested beside it, and a small chandelier cast a low, watery glow overhead.

It felt like a cathedral for surrender.

Aseeka stepped inside and exhaled.

She was still flushed, her thighs sticky with Byron's memory, her skin tingling where fingers had pressed, mouths had lingered. Her chest rose and fell as she leaned against the cool marble and let the silence settle.

A thick black towel was folded beside a bottle of body oil labeled Santal + Smoke.

She didn't think twice.

She took off the robes, slow and deliberate, letting it fall around her ankles. Her skin kissed the air, still marked with fingerprints and heat. She unclasped her bra, slid out of the lace, and stepped barefoot toward the shower.

The water turned on with the wave of her hand, a warm sheet of pressure cascading from above like liquid silk. She then grabbed a small brown box labeled "shower cap" off the counter and placed it on her head to protect her hair from the water. She had sweated it out a bit, but it was still intact. She would use the comb to put some strands back in place after she showered.

When she stepped in, it wasn't just about getting clean.

It was about coming back into herself. The effects of the Crave pill usually lasted about four hours, according to the clinical trials, and it had been in her system for two hours. The sensation she felt from her every move even elevated the shower experience.

Each drop whispered against her shoulders, rinsing away the urgency of sex, the noise of the party, the eyes, the hands. Her fingers ran over her body, not to arouse but to reconnect. She reflected on the sensation of Byron touching her. She became turned on again and knew she was ready for more excitement. It was like she couldn't resist it.

She tilted her head back, let the water run over her closed eyes, and exhaled.

And for a few minutes, in a room scented with eucalyptus and silence, Judge Aseeka Sinclair didn't have to be anything but human. She enjoyed her vulnerability and ability to take control of the situation between her and Byron. She thought about how he had fucked her brains out from the back and how good it felt. As the water trickled down her chest and washed away the soap from her lathered body, she paused and stood against the wall, thinking about what the rest of the night had in store.

She stepped out of the shower and grabbed a towel off the wall. Pulling off her shower cap, she looked directly ahead and admired herself in the mirror over the sink across from the shower. She then noticed the body oils, spray-on deodorant, and scented lotions in the far corner of the sink. She picked a warm vanilla-scented one; it was her next favorite scent after lavender. She rubbed a blend of the vanilla-scented oil and lotion over her hands and then all over her body. They even had melanin rose oil for your vagina. She placed a few drops directly on her pussy using the dropper in the bottle and then rubbed it in with her hands. Thanks to the pill, she was still wet, but she liked the smell of the rose oil, and it was soothing to her body. She then took her shower cap off and grabbed a rat-tail comb out of the basket on the sink. She inspected it to ensure it was clean and fixed her pixie to make it presentable.

She then put her tight, form-fitting corset dress back on; this time, she was pantiless thanks to Byron. And then stepped back into her heels. She was ready to go back to the party and enjoy the rest of the night. She stepped into the hallway and saw a man standing against the wall. A girl was giving down on her knees, giving him head. Aseeka could hear the slurping and thought, *get it, girl!*

The man was tall, chocolate-skinned, with broad shoulders, and masked. He was looking down at the woman with his hand on her head; he was enjoying her, and his moans confirmed that she knew what she was doing.

She looked at his biceps and thought, *wait a minute, I know that tattoo.*

And then she looked again at his face, but this time she saw him.

Damon.

Leaning back against the wall, just twenty feet down the corridor. One hand gripped the back of a woman's head, dark wig, red dress, knees on the floor like prayer, and his jaw was tight, mouth parted in a soft, involuntary groan that vibrated through the silence like bass without a beat.

He didn't even flinch at first. His eyes were closed.

But then he opened them.

And he saw her.

Aseeka. Standing there, exposed. Her heart thudded against her ribs like a fist trying to break through.

Their eyes locked.

Time stuttered.

For a moment, his lips moved; maybe her name, maybe a lie, maybe nothing at all. But the shock that snapped across her face swallowed whatever she meant to say.

Her breath caught sharply.

And then she turned.

Fast.

Her heels were pounding against the tile as she bolted back down the hallway, teeth clenched to keep the scream inside.

"Aseeka!" Damon called out behind her.

But she didn't stop.

She didn't want to hear the apology. Or the excuse. Or the guilt in his voice that would only piss her off more.

Because it wasn't just the act; it was what it meant.

Did he know she would be there?

Did he know Byron invited her there?

Her thoughts raced through her mind. What the fuck was happening? And for a moment, she almost felt her legs give out. Did he know she fucked Byron?

She had to find Tasha and get out of there ASAP. Or should she leave? Was he chasing after her?

She immediately darted into a private room and shut the door. Thank goodness it was empty. She stood against the door, trying to gather her thoughts.

She thought we were not official; he's not even my man. He's here just like I'm here. And his ass told me he was going to his son's tournament this weekend? Why the fuck was she panicking, she wasn't doing anything wrong, and neither was he, technically.

She gathered herself and decided to step back outside the private room and look for Tasha. It was now 3:15 a.m., and the party ended at 4 a.m. She wasn't in a head space to argue with Byron, so she decided to avoid him until she was of sound mind and body.

Aseeka stepped out of the room more composed, and went to the main room with the stage to look for Tasha. As soon as she entered the room, she spotted her. She was on the stage, gyrating to the sounds of Syrah's music like she was in a trance, her own little world. Aseeka could see how much she was enjoying herself and decided to let her be; she would confront her about trying to eat her pussy later, but tonight, she would just enjoy the vibe. She grabbed a glass of champagne from a passing tray, sat in an empty booth, and vibed to the music. She had enough excitement for one night; she would people-watch until it was time to go.

She focused on a corner where there was a nude man tied to an X-cross. The man was blindfolded, and both arms tied to each corner of the large wooden cross. His hands were handcuffed and dangling from chains. Behind him stood a woman holding a large black-and-purple flogger with a braided leather handle. She could tell the woman had already struck his bare exposed ass a few times by the red marks on his light-skinned ass. The woman stood in a leather dominatrix full-body suit that zipped up in the front. She was enjoying running the flogger up and down his ass and saying naughty things in his ear. She couldn't quite make out what the woman was saying as she tried to read her lips. But she could repeatedly make out the words *naughty boy* coming from her mouth. Aseeka watched enthusiastically and felt her pussy throb every time the woman hit the man on the ass with the flogger. She realized that this may be something she was into; she'd have to try it sometime, but not tonight.

Turning to focus back on the stage, she saw Tasha approaching the booth. She plopped down next to Aseeka, sweaty and breathing heavily.

She signaled for the server to bring her a drink, and the server hurried over to the table she grabbed a flute of champagne in each hand and looked at Aseeka, "I am wore the fuck out! I feel like I have been dancing for hours. How the fuck are you doing?"

Aseeka smiled from ear to ear, "I'm great; I saw Damon getting his dick sucked in the hallway. I ran into a private room and had to collect myself."

Tasha genuinely looked stunned, "No, the fuck you didn't, and how did I not know Damon was coming?"

Aseeka shrugged, "We can talk about it tomorrow, but for now, I want to finish enjoying the night."

They stayed in the booth and vibed to the music until the announcer came over the loudspeaker and introduced Byron to the stage.

Byron stood on the stage and smiled from ear to ear. "Did everybody have a good time tonight?"

You could hear several different confirmations being shouted loudly from the crowd. About 50-60 people were still left out of the 300 who were originally there at the start of the festivities. But people had slowly trickled out after getting their fantasies filled.

Byron looked around the room. "I genuinely want to thank you all for coming out tonight, and I especially want to thank my whole crew and support system, which helped make this happen."

Byron was naming everyone when he spotted Aseeka and Tasha in the booth and gave Tasha a special shoutout for helping with the event and the invitations. Tasha had employed Chanel's company to design the invitations, and they had done a damn good job!

After finishing his thank yous, he told everyone it was time to leave and motioned for Tasha to come to the front of the stage. Tasha got up and walked over to the stage, where he bent down and whispered something in her ear before kissing her on the lips.

Tasha returned to the booth, "I'm staying and helping Byron close up shop, and I'll head back to the hotel with him tonight. You can stay here with us if you want. Or our car is outside waiting for you, I can walk you to it if you need me to."

Aseeka had her fill of Byron and was ready to return to the hotel. I'm hoping not to run into Damon. "Girl, I'm good; I'll head outside to the car and text you when I return to the hotel."

Tasha signaled to one of the bouncers, who walked to the booth, "Make sure my friends get to our car safely, please, Mink.

The burly man, who looked like he'd knock a muthafucka out, nodded his head and walked Aseeka to the second-floor exit, making sure she collected her phone and then walked her to the car where the driver was waiting to take her back to the hotel. VIP vehicles lined up outside, waiting to take people to their destinations.

Aseeka was climbing into the car, about to shut the door, when she heard his voice behind her.

"Aseeka."

She turned, her face cool and her heartbeat steady.

Damon ran over to where she was and stood inside her car door so she couldn't shut it, jaw clenched, eyes hard. "That's what we're doing now?"

She cocked an eyebrow. "Excuse me?"

He stepped closer, voice low but sharp. "I saw you leaving the shower room. Who the fuck knows what you were washing off. He shook his head. "You out here like that?"

Aseeka smiled, slow and deadly. "Funny. I could say something similar about you and your condomless dick that that random woman was sucking. You were there too, Damon."

"That's not the point—"

"No," she cut him off. "The point is, we're not together. We've never been together. No labels. No rules. No expectations. That's what you wanted, right?"

His jaw flexed.

She leaned even closer, voice slicing through him like a blade. "You don't get to police me. Not my body. Not my choices. Not when you're looking for the same thing in the same building."

For a moment, he looked like he wanted to argue.

But he didn't.

Because she was right.

Without another word, she began to close the door as he backed away. His eyes focused on her, but he was completely silent. She could see anger, hurt, and intrigue on his face, which alarmed her slightly. She had enough excitement for the night and was ready to get some sleep.

She knew this wasn't the end, but she didn't have the strength or willingness to debate this with Damon.

She told the driver to pull off. "She didn't look back, not because she didn't care, but because her dignity was louder this time than his anger.

Chapter 19: Airspace and Aftermath

The jet hummed quietly beneath them as the Chicago skyline began to form in the distance, gray, cool, and unapologetically home. Aseeka sat by the window, wearing oversized shades, an oversized off-the-shoulder Chicago Cubs sweatshirt, royal blue leggings, and the kind of silence that said she was trying not to spiral.

Tasha sat across from her, curled into her seat with a blanket pulled halfway up her thigh and a mimosa she kept sipping but never really drank. The vibe between them was ... off. Something unfinished was floating between the leather seats and the altitude.

Aseeka finally broke it.

"You tried to fuck me."

Tasha's head snapped toward her, eyes wide.

Aseeka didn't raise her voice. She didn't need to. Her tone was calm. Stern. That slow-death kind of disappointment.

"I love you, Tasha. You know that," she said. "But don't ever try that shit again. Don't reach for me like that. Not in the middle of some scene. Not while I'm with a man or your man. Not ever."

Tasha's throat moved like she'd swallowed a hot coal. "I wasn't trying to disrespect you. I just, shit got blurry. It's you, 'Seeka. You walked in looking like temptation, and

Byron had fantasized about you for *years*. I just... I guess I wanted to know what that felt like. To share you."

Aseeka shook her head, not unkindly. "I'm not a *shared experience*, Tasha. I'm a whole fuckin person. And if we're really friends, like *real* friends, don't ever bring that moment up again. I've known you for over 30 years, and we have never … And don't bring up what happened with Byron either."

Tasha nodded slowly, biting her bottom lip. "Fair."

They both sat in silence for a beat.

Then Aseeka tilted her head and smiled. "That said ... Crave?"

Tasha's shoulders relaxed just a little. "That shit works, right?"

"Girl," Aseeka laughed, "that shit is *the truth*. You are about to be a whole mogul out here. I'm so glad I invested. I don't care what you say, you tapped into something big. Women, men, and everyone else, gon' be thanking you in secret group chats for decades."

Tasha grinned. "That's the goal."

"And despite the drama," Aseeka added, "that party was wild. I'd ... I'd do it again."

Tasha raised an eyebrow. "You sure?"

"I'm not saying I'd fuck your man again," Aseeka smirked, "but I am saying ... I might be a little more interested in exploring some kinky shit. Soft rope. Open doors. A blindfold, whip, handcuffs, or two. I mean, Damon and I already explore that kind of shit, but I witnessed a new level last night!"

Tasha gasped, hand to chest. "Look at God."

They laughed loudly, shoulders finally dropping as they leaned into the moment. But then Aseeka's voice dropped again, more serious this time.

"Honestly, friend, how do you feel about what happened between Byron and me?"

Tasha paused, thoughtful.

"Honestly? I was ... surprised. But I'm not mad. I know how he looks at you. And you have grown. I knew what this trip could turn into when he said your name. What pissed me off wasn't y'all, it was me thinking I could handle it better than I did."

Aseeka nodded, grateful for the honesty. "You sure?"

"I'm good," Tasha said. "And let's be real, you looked *happy* at that moment. Glowing. That man made you cum three times, didn't he?"

"Four," Aseeka whispered with a smirk.

Tasha clutched her pearls and squealed. "Bitch!"

They were still laughing when Aseeka's face shifted.

"Oh. And you know Damon tried to come at me on some clown shit?"

Tasha blinked. "No …"

"Damon."

"Nooo."

"Ran up on me at the club, trying to play angry boyfriend. Meanwhile, he had somebody's throat on his dick twenty minutes before I saw him."

"Hypocrite *ass!*" Tasha yelled.

"Girl. He's lucky I didn't slap the fake, non-spoken monogamy agreement outta him. Talking about how he couldn't believe I was there. Boy, you had your whole balls out on the second floor. Miss me with that bullshit."

Tasha was howling now. "You better *not* give him the energy. That shouldn't even be a conversation."

"It's not," Aseeka said, reaching for her phone. "I'm over it."

The pilot's voice came through the intercom. "Ladies, we'll be landing in ten minutes. Please return your seats upright and prepare to return to reality."

Tasha rolled her eyes. "Ugh. Reality."

They grabbed their phones and turned them off airplane mode as the plane descended onto the runway.

Ding.

Ding. Ding. Ding. Dingdingdingdingding.

Aseeka's home screen was flooded with missed calls, voicemails, and texts.

Chanel (4 missed calls)
Malik (2 voicemails)
Brielle (5 messages)
Gwerls Group Chat (49 unread messages)

Tasha's phone buzzed just as wildly. Her smile faded as she scrolled. Then her lips parted. Her hand covered her mouth.

Aseeka's heart started pounding.

She opened the group chat.

> Chanel: Y'all need to get to the hospital. It's Syd."
> Brielle: "The Center for Care & Discovery. ASAP."
> Malik: "Please call me. It's bad."
> Chanel: "I'm not okay."

The laughter evaporated. The altitude suddenly felt suffocating.

Tasha whispered, "Oh my god ... something happened to Sydney."

Aseeka looked out the window, fists clenched, stomach twisting.

Suddenly, the landing couldn't come fast enough.

Chapter 20: When the Music Stops

The doors to the ICU waiting room hissed open, and the Gwerls stepped in like a storm had finally touched down.

Aseeka Tasha, still in their airport clothes, eyes swollen from lack of sleep. Chanel, Brielle, and Malik were already there, faces drawn, energy flat. Everyone was sitting against the wall in a line of chairs in the waiting room. Beside them, Sydney's parents sat motionless. Their mother's hand clutched a damp tissue. Her eyes are red and swollen from all the tears she has shed. Their father stared at the muted TV screen as it owed him an explanation for the unimaginable.

They all looked up as the group entered, but no one smiled. Not even Malik.

Chanel stood first, voice shaking. "They're ... they're not gonna make it."

Aseeka blinked. "What?"

Malik swallowed hard. "He shot them, 'Seeka. Four times. In the chest. The head. Their stomach. They were defending themself, but ..." he broke off.

Brielle added softly, "They revived them four times. But ... the doctors say there's no brain activity. No response. They keep them alive long enough for us to say goodbye."

"They made us promise," Chanel whispered, eyes full again. "If anything ever happened, do not let them stay like that. They said they didn't want to live hooked to wires; they wanted to be or go."

The TV in the waiting room flashed with a breaking news banner:

"South Side Man Charged in Brutal Shooting of Black Trans Individual"

Sydney's face appeared, radiant and full of life, with their guitar in their hand, sitting under a hanging mic in the studio.

Then it cut to Shawn's mugshot, eyes swollen shut, lip busted, jaw bruised.

"Police have confirmed the suspect, Shawn Gregory, was arrested at the scene. He is currently being charged with second-degree murder."

The room pulsed with a mix of rage and despair.

Aseeka barely heard them calling her name as she stormed down the hall. She pushed past nurses, past protocol, and past fear until she reached the ICU door marked with Sydney's name.

And then she saw them.

Sydney.

So still. Tubes in their mouth, machines beeping. Their face was swollen, and their lips were cracked, a bruise on their temple. Bullet wounds marred their beautiful skin, and their crown was wrapped in gauze.

Aseeka gasped, hand flying to her mouth. Her knees nearly buckled.

This wasn't supposed to happen.

A doctor appeared behind her. "I'm so sorry. They've been on life support since Friday. Their organs have begun shutting down. There's nothing more we can do."

Sydney's mother appeared behind Aseeka and put her hand on her shoulder, "I know this is hard, but we kept her alive so y'all could say goodbye. Please, Aseeka, just ... . She immediately began sobbing and fell into her husband's arms.

Aseeka nodded through tears. "Ok, give us a minute."

One by one, they entered the room. The Gwerls. Their family. Their tribe.

Malik stepped forward first, voice barely above a whisper. "You were magic, Syd. You changed how I saw myself. I swear to God, your legacy ... it ain't going nowhere. I'll make sure the world knows your name."

Chanel wiped her eyes. "You taught me grace, baby. You taught me how to walk into a room like it owed me something. Who's goin' to make me laugh now? All those times when I needed you, you always showed up. Never judged, always comforted me. Always"

Brielle leaned over and kissed Syd's hand. "You always said glitter was a spiritual gift. You were right. You were the sparkle we needed."

Tasha looked at them, shoulders trembling. "I'm gonna get some of the homies in County to fuck him up good. I don't care what anybody says. He gon' feel it. Just like we are going to feel your absence …"

She broke down before she finished and ran out sobbing. Her eyes were so soaked with tears that she could barely see in front of her.

Malik followed her.

Then it was just Aseeka.

She walked to the bedside, took Sydney's hand, and let it all fall.

"You were the bravest soul I ever met. When we first met, you became my protector, a true image of authenticity, love, fierceness, and everything in between. You showed up when it was hard. You lived louder than most people ever will. You didn't deserve this." Her voice cracked. "And I'm so, so sorry we couldn't protect you. I'm sorry that we live in a world that thinks you don't deserve to be protected, but I will work to change all of that. I promise."

Tears streamed down her cheeks.

"I promise you, we will make sure he pays on everything I got. And I'll spend the rest of my life making this world less cruel to the next you. I swear it."

She bent down and kissed Sydney's forehead, the only place without a bandage.

The doctor returned. "Are you ready?"

No one answered.

But everyone nodded.

They unplugged the machine.

And just like that, the beeping slowed.

Stopped.

Flatline.

Tasha stood outside the door, sobbing into Malik's chest. She couldn't bear to see them go.

Inside, the rest of them stood in silence, shattered but present. They watched as Syd's body became lifeless. As the air completely left their chest.

Sydney's light had left the room.

But their power? Their voice? Their beauty?

That would never die.

Chapter 21: Smoke in the Sky

The air outside the hospital was colder than it had any right to be. The kind of cold that hits the chest, sharp and mean, like grief trying to wear a trench coat. The Gwerls stepped out of the Center for Care and Discovery in a silence that screamed.

Nobody said a word.

Not at first.

Aseeka's eyes were rimmed red. Her jaw locked. Her whole body vibrated with restraint like she might scream, throw a glass vase, or drop to her knees and never get up, but she didn't know which.

Tasha's hands were balled into fists so tight her acrylics bit her palms. She was the first to break the quiet.

"I want that muthafucka dead."

"Same," Chanel said, voice hollow.

Brielle, always the calm one, wrapped her coat tighter. "We need to be smart. We need to move."

"I don't give a damn about smart," Tasha snapped. "Syd's gone. They're *gone*, and he's sitting in County with a fucking cot and three meals!"

"We are not letting this fade," Malik added, his voice low and seething. "Not this time. Syd's name gon' ring."

They stood in a tight circle on the sidewalk, the streetlights washing their faces in soft gold. Cars passed. Life kept moving like it hadn't just lost someone unforgettable.

Brielle's phone buzzed. A Twitter notification.

> @_justice4syd: "Black trans woman shot and killed in Hyde Park by a cis male partner. Say their name: Sydney Love. #JusticeForSyd #ProtectTransLives"

It was already starting.

And it wouldn't be enough.

"Vigil," Chanel said. "Tomorrow. Millennium Park. I'll coordinate with Syd's mom."

"Press," Tasha added. "I'm calling everybody. Local. National. I got people in LA, too. And I'm not just talking blogs, I want fucking CNN."

Aseeka finally spoke. Her voice didn't tremble. It sliced. "I'm calling Judge Whitaker. I want an emergency sit-down with the Commission on Equity. I want Syd's name on every docket dealing with hate crime and LGBTQ protections this quarter."

They all turned to her.

"I'm not just a judge," she said. "I'm a Black, furious woman with a fucking gavel. And I'm done whispering."

Malik stepped closer to her. "What do you need from us?"

"Truth," she said. "Testimonies. Soundbites. Photos. Everything that proves Syd was loved, brilliant, and alive. It's not just another headline or hashtag. Not just a statistic."

Tasha wiped her face with the back of her hand. "You got it. I'll get footage from their old performances. Every time they hosted Pride, every speech, every damn slay."

"Let's burn this shit down," Chanel said. "Then rebuild something better."

They all nodded.

At that moment, they weren't just friends grieving.

They were architects of a legacy.

They were Black, queer, femme, and trans warriors, wounded but not broken.

And tomorrow?

The whole city would hear Sydney Love's name.

Chapter 22: Love Don't Die Easy

The church hummed like it had breath.

Beacon of Light Unity Church sat on the corner of 59th and Ellis, wrapped in rainbow flags and blooming white lilies. The sanctuary was packed, pews lined with families, elders, activists, drag queens, trans people, poets, queer youth, aunties in wide-brimmed hats, and row after row of people who Sydney Love had touched.

The choir swayed in royal purple robes, their harmonies soft as cotton and heavy with sorrow. The organ moaned beneath them, a soul-deep sound that wrapped around every bone in the building.

The casket sat at the front, closed, sleek, and covered in white roses. A glitter-dusted black sash was draped across it, with bold gold letters spelling: "LIVED LOUD."

The air inside was thick with incense, tears, and silence that only showed up when spirits were present.

Aseeka sat in the front row, tissue pressed to her face, locs pinned beneath a black beret. Next to her, Tasha, Chanel, Brielle, and Malik held hands, their eyes swollen but proud. The men, Markee, Kenneth, and Sydney's father, Mr. Love, stood in solemn support behind them.

When the pastor stepped forward, the room quieted like the sky before thunder.

"We are here," she said, voice calm and unapologetic, "not because Sydney died, but because Sydney lived. And they did so beautifully."

Snaps. Amens. Applause.

Then came the tribute. A moment so personal, piercing, tore through the entire room.

Four artists took the pulpit, two singers, a pianist, and a trans male rapper with eyes full of fire, and performed the last song Sydney ever wrote: "Hiding." They sang it like a prayer. A testimony. A funeral dirge that curled around every heart like ribbon.

> *"I ain't hiding no more. I ain't shrinking,*
> *folding, breaking no more.*
> *You gon' see me, feel me, hear me, even if my*
> *body ain't here no more."*

People wept. Sobbed. Collapsed into each other's arms. The music didn't end, it just dissolved into silence.

Then, slowly, people began to rise. The choir hummed again. The casket was rolled down the center aisle. The congregation stood in reverence.

Until the air shifted.

And the bullshit arrived.

A dusty green pickup truck screeched to a stop just outside the church gates, tires kicking up gravel like it had a damn message to deliver. Five or six anti-trans protestors jumped out, white, sunburnt, angry, and held up signs that read:

"TRANS LIES DON'T MATTER!"
"GOD HATES SINNERS."
"YOU CAN'T CHANGE GOD'S DESIGN."

The Gwerls froze. Tasha blinked. Malik whispered, "They gotta be out they whole-ass mind."

Before anyone could think, Markee was already on the move.

He flew down the church stairs like a man possessed, hollering, "DO YOU KNOW WHERE THE FUCK YOU AT, NIGGA?!" before laying a mean right hook into the jaw of the first protestor.

BOW! Man dropped like groceries.

One of the protestors tried to jump on Markee's back.

Bad choice.

Kenneth running behind Markee, grabbed the man mid-air and body-slammed him to the concrete like WWE was paying him.

Brielle, screaming, "NOT TODAY, BITCH!" swung her purse like a wrecking ball, smacking another protestor across the face with a heel sticking out the side. Blood. Feathers. Justice.

Aseeka and Malik kicked a big, red-faced protestor who'd slipped on a hymnal and hit the ground. "Y'all really tried it!" Malik shouted between kicks. "Y'all *really* thought today was the day!"

And then Mr. Love, Syd's father, stepped forward.

Quiet. Focused. Deadly.

A Krav Maga master in full grieving father mode, he snapped one man's arm behind his back and popped his shoulder clean out of the socket like it was a Lego. "My child was a warrior. Y'all just brought sticks to a war."

The church security, finally snapping into action, flooded out and pulled the Gwerls and husbands back inside, breathless, bruised, but triumphant. The church doors slammed loudly behind them with a loud clasp. Security positioned themselves in front of the door, thankful all the attendees did not have the chance to exit the church for the brawl. It would have been out of control.

Outside the protestors were picking themselves up and fleeing from the scene where the ass whopping had ensued.

Inside, everyone paused. Looked at each other.

And then, out of nowhere, Malik laughed.

A deep, belly-shaking laugh.

"You know damn well Syd would've done the SAME shit. And Mr. Love, I see you still got it!"

The room erupted. Laughter. Tears. Relief.

Tasha fixed her ponytail. "They probably up there in the VIP of the afterlife, clapping like, 'THAT'S how you ride.'"

Everyone straightened themselves out, fixed edges and skirts, and made their way back outside to the limos. The energy was different now, lighter, stronger, rooted.

The Gwerls piled into the limo with Sydney's family, their men nearby.

Markee leaned into Chanel and whispered, "Bae ... I think I wanna start a security company."

Chanel blinked. "What?"

"I'm serious. I got hands. And I have a purpose now. I wanna protect our people. I don't mind knocking a nigga out if it means keeping somebody like Syd safe. You know, I don't know much about the LGBTQ community, but I have people in my family who I love and who identify. That moment breathed a bit of life and purpose back into me."

She looked at him, really looked, and for the first time in months, her heart softened.

"I'm proud of you. Let's go build your dream, baby."

The limo pulled away and headed for the burial site.

At the cemetery, the wind carried the sound of birds and hushed prayers. They stood around the casket as it lowered into the earth, each dropping a rose. A crystal. A memory.

Aseeka whispered as they lowered the casket, "Rest loud, baby."

Sydney Love was gone.

But not forgotten.

Not ever.

Chapter 23: All Rise

The courthouse was quieter than usual that morning. Not in sound, but in energy. The kind of stillness that felt like the building was holding its breath. Even the walls knew grief had walked in wearing heels and a fitted blazer.

Aseeka stepped off the elevator and into her chambers, her face light but clean, like armor. Her black blouse was tucked into high-waisted pants, sharp enough to slice, soft enough to comfort. She was still carrying the weekend's weight, but she carried it like a judge. Like a queen. Like a woman who knew the power of silence.

Ms. Ellie stood at the desk sipping tea and watching her with warm, wise eyes. Her energy felt warm and welcoming as it often did, but this time with an intentional focus on Aseeka. She knew exactly what Aseeka needed to hear and was ready to deliver a much-needed message.

"You showed up," Ms. Ellie said. "I knew you would, you always do, for everybody."

"Had to," Aseeka replied, voice low.

Ms. Ellie set down her mug. "Loss will gut you, honey. But it'll also grow you."

Aseeka sat on the edge of her desk, head heavy, heart fuller than it wanted.

"Shakespeare once said," Ms. Ellie began, "*Give sorrow words. The grief that does not speak whispers o'er the fraught heart and bids it break.*"

Aseeka blinked, chest tight.

"That was his way of saying what Black women have been telling each other for centuries," Ms. Ellie continued. "Don't hold it in, baby. Speak your pain before it swallows you."

That quote wrapped itself around her like a shawl: elegant, aged, and necessary.

"Thank you, Ms. Ellie," Aseeka whispered.

Ms. Ellie nodded and stepped out, leaving the door cracked.

Moments later, there was a knock.

Ms. Ellie opened her door and announced that her father, David, was there. She gave Aseeka a look as if to say, "Take the damn meeting, you need it." Shortly after Aseeka gestured for her to let him through, he stepped into the room, broad and composed, with eyes full of decades of words he hadn't spoken. He removed his hat and stood lowly by the door, unsure if he belonged.

"I heard about your friend," he said.

Aseeka nodded once, lips pressed tight. "What do you want, Daddy?"

He took a breath. "I wanted to tell you what happened to Marcus Voss. But I need to know if this is a good time. I don't mean to cause you any more pain than you are already experiencing my child."

She didn't speak. Just stared.

David moved slowly to the chair across her desk, placing a worn envelope on the surface. "Your mother and he both attended Northwestern together. They had a sex-ed class together. He was obsessed with her. He stalked your mother for months. Left her shaking. One night, I caught him outside the house, weapon in hand. I confronted him. We fought. He told her what he was going to do. And I," he stopped, looked at his hands. "I snapped."

Aseeka's heart pounded.

"I don't regret protecting her. I regret leaving you to think I didn't love you enough to say goodbye."

He slid the envelope forward. "There's a file. Proof. Names. Timelines. I want you to have it because they're reopening his old assault cases. I know your mother made you promise never to look at my case, but I think you need to see it, especially since I learned about this Garvin case on your desk. His brother, right? I had a few of my lady friends go to his office once I found out he had a practice on the South Side. I didn't trust him either; he tried hard to cover for his brother. Plus, I knew eventually he'd slip up, and a few years ago, he did. You see, a predator always needs prey to feed their urge, and finally, I sent the right bait. I called one of my side pieces, Loretta, who I knew worked at the office, and she told me that he was a little off and would keep her eyes open for me. I told her my friend would be coming to look out for her, and she did. He got too friendly with this patient, and she went to the cops. It's what started the investigation into him and his practice.

Her father said it with a smile that pissed her off. Because what did she mean, side pieces? She knew her daddy had cheated on her mother back in the day but never had any hard proof. But that was the least of her concerns; he had sought to protect her, even from behind bars, and that shit hit differently.

"He had almost 25 victims come forward so far. Can you believe that mess? Anyway, I was ready to kill the whole family because I could feel something was wrong. When I found out your mother had been his client, I asked her if he had tried anything. She assured me he had not, and she felt foolish for sending her daughter to that monster. I could hear the hurt in her voice when she said you seemed different when you came back from his office. She was somewhat disturbed when she called you to see how the visit went, and she could tell something was up by your voice. She told me she would ask you more when you got home. I told her to leave it alone. You were always the type to tell us something when you were damn good and ready, and if you didn't, we knew not to push it. You are stubborn and a control freak, just like me."

Aseeka was stunned, "What are you trying to tell me, Daddy?"

David's face was dead serious as he stared at his daughter, "I know a few of the women who turned him in. Let's just say they all owed me a favor. I took care of their baby daddies and a few of their family members behind bars."

Aseeka's eyes were beginning to water up, wondering how her father knew and did all of this from prison and how her mother secretly knew something but never said anything. She realized that they were trying to save her from the shame. At the same time, her mother covered her own. If they had pressed, she would have blown up, so she appreciated that they never did, especially as she grappled with whether or not she enjoyed the moment. Even though it was wrong, and she had never consented! It made sense that when she told her mother she was switching gynecologists immediately after the visit, her mother did not make a fuss and switched. And how her Daddy was running a sting operation from the gotdamn prison.

Her father stared at her in silence. He knew it was starting to come together in her head. He said sternly, "I planned to kill him when I got out, but after you spend almost a few decades in prison, you know it's a place you never want to go back to, so I had to be smart. I made many friends there, from guards to men who never see the light of day. I ran that muthafucka, even as an inmate. There are a lot of people in there who owe me favors. They are waiting on him to come on in, let's just say they got something for that ass, literally! Rapists don't do too well behind them prison walls. So, I want you to help me ensure he gets the time he deserves. But we must be smart; you can't try this case."

The idea of revenge, without a conflict of interest that could harm her, created a sense of joy for Aseeka. Her father had people on the inside, and she had the right connections to ensure he would get what he deserved. She made a mental note to speak with Damon about speaking to Judge Whitaker. The judge was a good judge, but he was a member of the good ol' boys club. The request would be better received if it came from Damon. She didn't earn the Chief Judge position without being strategic; as a woman, she had to be or else.

Her father continued with this well-thought-out plan, "I know you know what a conflict of interest is, baby girl. And I don't want you to harm everything you have worked so hard for out of avenging me or your mother. I want you to hand off the case. It'll destroy your reputation if you don't. People won't care that I saved your mother. They'll care that you're my daughter."

It hurt because it was true. She could never tell her father about the assault she encountered at the hands of the doctor, and he would for sure kill him, too, and end up right back in prison. She also gained a new sense of respect for the old man; he was still smart and knew how to run shit! She thought this would be a secret she would keep from her family and take to the grave. Well, now that she knew her parents knew, it released a burden off of her shoulders. Plus, they would never speak of it to her siblings. They had enough of their own shit to worry about in life.

He stood.

"I'll love you until I'm dust, baby girl. Whatever you decide, I trust you."

He kissed the top of her head.

And just like that, he was gone.

Before she could catch her breath or gather her thoughts, another knock.

Ms. Ellie opened the door, "You sure are popular this morning; Judge Damon Clark is here to see you, she said with a smirk.

She groaned, immediately irritated as he stepped through the door and closed it behind him. What a fucking morning. Who did he think he was dropping by her gotdamn office like nothing had happened? She couldn't wait to hear what his ass had to say. She hadn't heard from him since LA. He had reached out a few times, but she was busy with Sydney's services and working on building a platform rooted in justice for her friend.

"You've got 20 minutes."

He stepped in, his suit slightly wrinkled and his eyes raw. He looked like regret and fine-ass foolishness wrapped in Burberry cologne.

"I fucked up," he said, cutting right to the chase. Damon wasn't one for small talk; she remembered she loved that about him. "I shouldn't have come at you sideways. I was mad, but I was wrong. I saw you leaving that room at the party and realized maybe I don't want the traditional life. Marriage again, no. But ... I want *you.* I want the real. The raw. The truth. I want to build something real, with pleasure, with intention, with *us.*"

She raised a brow. "You're asking me to be in a kinky-ass life partnership?"

"I'm asking you to build a kingdom alongside me, baby. One where the walls moan, and the floors know our names."

That did it.

Sensing his voice's sincerity and passion, she stood off her desk and walked over to him. She had missed him, wanted to be vulnerable with him, and underneath it all, she was in love with Damon. She was realizing how short life was, and she wanted to live it vibrantly, kinky as fuck, and free!

She grabbed him by the tie, yanked him into her office bathroom, and slammed the door behind them.

The sex was urgent and overdue.

Hot. Sloppy. Heated.

He pressed her against the cold tile wall, her legs wrapped around his waist, his mouth devouring her neck as she unzipped his pants with practiced fury. Damon ferociously removed her pants and ripped open her blouse. She had extra clothes in the closet. She knew she'd be fine. She had pulled off his suit jacket and opened his button-up underneath, exposing his chest.

She looked him dead in his eyes, "Spank me, Daddy, she said to him before she kissed him intensely.

Damon didn't say a word; he removed his jacket and sat it on the door hook; he turned around, immediately flipped her around, and instructed her to bend over and hold on to the sink. Aseeka standing half naked in an open blouse with her titties hanging, she did not resist.

He stood behind her and kicked her feet apart while he caressed her ass cheeks with both hands. He took a step back to make room to build momentum for his strong ass hands to smack her ass. The first smack on her right cheek was intense, but she could tell he was holding back. She felt a slight sting from the pain but more pleasure than anything, and that caused her pussy to start throbbing as she could feel the juices forming between her walls. Although she didn't have a lot of ass, she had enough for it to jiggle. And she knew how to make it clap if necessary.

Before she could say anything, she felt another smack, this one more fierce, a bit louder.

Damon was standing straight up behind her; she could see him in the mirror above the sink as she bent over it, still wearing her heels, "You like that shit, huh," he said, staring at her in the mirror. Tell Daddy how much you like it."

And before she could say anything, he smacked her ass again, a bit harder, more intense.

Aseeka could feel the adrenaline rushing through her body. She was so turned on by his dominance that she wanted to scream, but all that came out was a whisper of, "Yes, da—."

Before she could finish, Damon had shoved his index and middle finger of his right hand, in her pussy from the back and was pushing them in and out slowly, "Shut the fuck up."

She could tell he was disciplining her for the weekend in LA but also wanted to remind her that he was that dude and not to play with him. It turned her on like crazy. Her pussy was completely drenched now. Damon knew precisely how to find her G-spot with his long-ass fingers. He could feel her breathing growing more intensely, and he knew her body well enough to know when she was about to cum.

He knew he was pressing directly on G-spot. Watching her in the mirror, unable to close her mouth, completely submissive to him, was sending him, and just before she was about to erupt, he pulled his fingers out and rammed his fully erect dick into her pussy from the back.

Aseeka was trying her best not to scream out as his dick stroke was fierce and completely filled her pussy with pleasure. Damon was still staring at her in the mirror as he smacked her ass. He knew she was his, "This is my pussy, and don't you ever give it to anybody else!" He smacked her ass again to the point where her ass cheeks were slightly red.

Aseeka erupted, cum shooting out of her pussy and down her legs, "Yes, Daddy, it's yours." She loved it when he took control and made it known she was his. The deep feeling of being wanted and loved connected the emotions to the moment.

Before she could move, Damon had gently started rubbing his dick against her asshole. He slowly pushed the tip in and out. They had done anal before, it wasn't anything new, but it still took her by surprise. He didn't like his ass being played with, but he loved putting anal beads in her ass, thumbs, fingers, his dick, whatever!

She looked at him in the mirror and smiled. Letting him know that it was OK to proceed. She opened the mirror, went into the medicine cabinet behind it, pulled out a small travel-sized bottle of K-Y Jelly, and handed it to him. She wanted to feel him in every part of her body. Fuck it, she was coming in her soft girl era and was happy to exist in it with Damon.

Damon was smiling ear to ear as he watched her grab the bottle, "Turn around and rub it on my dick," he said with mischief seriousness. Never breaking eye contact with the mirror.

Aseeka looked surprised but excited. She stood up and turned slowly, squeezing some of the jelly in her hand while looking him in the eye. She had to move slowly as her knees were still recovering from her orgasm. She gently began to rub it on Damon's dick while he slightly moaned. Kissing him intensely as she rubbed his dick. She loved looking into his eyes as he moaned, knowing she was the catalyst for his pleasure. Stroke by stroke, she lathered his dick in the lubricant until it was completely covered.

Damon was so turned on he grabbed her by the arm, turned her back around quickly, and bent her back over the sink.

She was panting before he even got inside.

Again spreading her legs by kicking her feet apart, he slowly inserted his dick in her asshole inch by inch until it was halfway in, and he slowly began to increase his strokes as she became more relaxed.

Aseeka wanted to cry and moan at the same time as she felt Damon's hands on her hips, guiding her over his dick. He was so deep, and then he grabbed by the hair. Her short pixie was just long enough for him to grab a hand full of hair as she could feel the intensity of his strokes picking up and became wetter at the sound of her ass cheeks smacking against his hard body.

"Say it," he growled, pushing deep.

"That you're still an arrogant asshole?"

He thrust harder.

She gasped. "Fuck, you feel so …"

"I love you," he grunted. "And I'm never letting you go."

"I love you too," she moaned.

Feeling his stroke began to slow, she knew exactly when he was about to cum.

"Don't you dare nut inside of me," she gasped.

"He said slowly, "I wouldn't dream of it, Judge."

They moved like fire and smoke, no rhythm, just heat. Her hands clenched the sync. His hand covered her mouth when she almost screamed.

They came together.

Collapsed with each other.

Panting.

Spent.

Silent.

In the stillness, he kissed her temple.

"Partners?" he whispered.

"Don't test me, Damon."

He smirked. "That's a yes."

She rolled her eyes, wiped herself down, and fixed her clothes.

When they emerged from the bathroom, both had taken the time to fix themselves together. Aseeka, now in a red dress, pulled from her closet and curled her hair.

She looked at Damon, sitting on the adult-sized bean bag, who was straightening his slacks. As he watched her fix her makeup, she said, "I need a couple of favors."

"What's that, anything for you, my love," he said playfully.

"I need to hand the Garvin case off to Judge Whitaker or another judge; it's a conflict of interest for me.

Damon looked puzzled but didn't want to question her after their time together, "Ok, I'll speak with him; what else?"

Her jaw tightened, and he could see the seriousness in her face, "I need to know who the presiding judge is over Sydney's case and make sure I share … my thoughts."

Damon knew precisely what she meant, and he was on it. He liked it when she depended on him, and since he couldn't attend the funeral due to the boy's basketball tourney, he was happy to help. "Let's make sure we fry ol' boy!"

They were official partners now and in it together. She finished applying her red lipstick and walked over to him, and pulled him up by the hand; you gotta go; I got shit to do, and so do you, my love.

She opened the door and walked him out, and he kissed her gently before exiting the office, "I'll get that done and be in touch. See you tonight."

Ms. Ellie was sitting at her desk, sipping her tea with a knowing smile.

"Told you," she said softly, smirking, "loss grows you."

Aseeka closed her office door behind her.

Her phone buzzed. It was a message from Byron.

> Byron: What's good?

And for the first time in a long time, she didn't feel like something was missing.

She felt … chosen.

To Be Continued……..

Made in the USA
Columbia, SC
25 April 2025

57161174R00130